Acclaim for Allison Burnett's
The Escape of Malcolm Poe

"Where the domestic meets the comic grotesque. John Cheever as told by Nathanael West."
—Dan Fante, author of *Point Doom* and *Chump Change*

"Underneath Allison Burnett's characteristic dark hilarity beats a truthful and tender heart. A sensational read!"
—Jillian Lauren, author *Some Girls: My Life in a Harem*

"A virtuoso rendering of what it means to be fifty years old. With the grace of Nabokov and the intelligence of Saul Bellow, Burnett has a written a novel that youngsters should read to see what's in store, the middle-aged to have their feelings and experiences validated, and the elderly to remember. A remarkable achievement by a remarkable author."
—Eric Miles Williamson, author of *East Bay Grease* and *Welcome to Oakland*

"Salinger for big boys."
—Gigi Levangie, author of *Starter Wife* and *Seven Deadlies*

"At turns acerbic and buoyant, vicious and surprisingly tender, Allison Burnett treats the subject of midlife dread and collapse with astonishing incisiveness. Burnett's novel manages the delicious trick of being simultaneously evanescent and harrowing. It's also really fucking funny."
—Matthew Spektor, author of *That Summertime Sound* and *American Dream Machine*

"With pitch-perfect humor, *The Escape of Malcolm Poe* celebrates and exalts the absurdity of the human condition. Allison Burnett is as insightful as he is funny — and he is very, very funny."
—Sue Halpern, author of *A Dog Walks Into a Nursing Home* and *Can't Remember What I Forgot*

"Allison Burnett's prose is a near-impossible crossroads where the resplendent meets the acerbic. A wholly original voice that captures the Ulyssean wanderlust at the root of the post-modern white male's decline."
—David Kukoff, author of *Children of the Canyon*

"Here is the rapier wit, the unreliable narrator, and the high speed page-turning we have come to expect from Burnett. But his work h̶̶̶̶̶̶̶̶̶̶̶̶̶̶̶̶̶ ̶̶̶̶̶̶̶̶̶̶̶̶̶̶'ous and lyrical with every book. Open it an̶̶̶̶̶̶̶̶̶̶̶̶̶̶̶̶ ̶̶̶̶̶̶̶̶̶̶̶̶̶̶̶̶hat you won't do is stop reading." —Dr. Micha̶̶ ̶̶̶̶̶̶̶̶̶̶̶̶̶̶̶̶ ̶̶̶̶̶̶̶̶̶̶̶̶̶̶̶̶d *Group Meditation*

"Malcolm himself is a wonde̶̶̶ ̶̶̶̶̶̶̶̶̶̶̶̶̶̶̶̶ ̶̶̶̶̶̶̶̶̶̶̶̶̶̶̶̶ ̶̶̶̶̶̶̶̶̶̶1ehow persistently worthy not only of the reade̶̶ ̶̶̶̶̶̶̶̶̶̶̶̶̶̶̶̶ ̶̶̶̶̶̶̶̶̶̶̶̶̶̶̶̶ ̶̶̶̶̶1 may sometimes find yourself reading another ̶p̶a̶g̶e̶, and another page after that, almost in spite of yourself, but I can't imagine you'll be able to tear yourself away. This is fearless stuff."
—Benjamin Dreyer, author of *The Last Word*

THE
ESCAPE
OF
MALCOLM POE

a novel
by
Allison Burnett

writers tribe books

Published by Writers Tribe Books
www.writerstribebooks.com

Book design by Amy Inouye
Cover photograph by Don Davis Photography

Published in the United States of America

ISBN 978-1-937746-19-3

For Zalman King & Patricia Knop

"To become a spectator of one's own life is to escape the suffering of life."

—OSCAR WILDE

BOOK ONE

As I walked up the Craters' driveway, I hugged Louise close, which made her smile. I used to love that smile. Taking our coats, Earl Crater said that we were the only couple who hadn't missed a single one of their New Year's Eve bashes since the tradition began two decades ago. He waited for me to beam with pride. I felt sick to the soul. How had it come to this? Year after year, celebrating hope and renewal with a pair of pitiful, old drunks.

What a debacle they are. Earl staggering to the grave, trying not to spill his gimlet. Estelle is worse—trembling hands, yellow teeth, hacking cough. If it were up to me, we'd have stayed home and stared at bad television, but seeing as how the Craters' daughter killed our son, God forbid we should refuse them anything. That's actually how Louise sees the world. She worries incessantly about the feelings of others, and yet for all she knows the Craters drowned their guilt long ago and invite us only out of obligation.

I made a beeline for the bar, where I summoned small talk with three old gents in blue blazers. What is it about elderly WASPs and dandruff? Is it genetic or learned? With the help of much champagne and a postcard view of the sound, I feigned an interest in golf and college football while they pretended to care where my youngest had applied to school. When the topic switched, as it inevitably does, to the evil of the Democrats, I began to count boats, buoys, and blinking lights. Soon I was tipsy and envious of every sailor who had ever been lost at sea.

During the countdown to midnight, Louise hustled over for her big holiday kiss. I smiled down at her with damp eyes, as though another year together were all the happiness I could ever wish for. Thank God there were no mirrors around. Sometimes I catch my reflection at moments like these, and I'm speechless with shame. I shudder at how unconvincing I am. Why doesn't she see it and slap me across the face?

The party dispersed quickly, everyone eager to return to his comfy bed, one year closer to the worms.

The fog was heavy driving home, and I was feeling drunk. Phantoms swam across the headlights. Louise tried not to laugh as I savaged our hosts. "Mal, be nice," she begged. "They don't have much longer. Please. Can't you be nice?" I told her that I could not. I killed the engine, glided up the driveway, and jumped out. I opened the front door as quickly and silently as I could, hoping to catch Karen and her new best friend Maya smoking pot and kissing with tongues. But, alas, they were crunching down giant pretzels and flipping through a coffee table book on rain forests. I suppose there's an upside to having a serious, prudish daughter, but it's so obvious that she's a lesbian, I wish she'd just make the announcement and get the party started.

After a few minutes of holiday chitchat, mother and daughter retired upstairs and I followed little Maya to her hybrid. She said it was unnecessary, but I said no, no, you can never be too careful, even the best neighborhoods have rapists. She glanced back at me as though I were one of them.

As she crawled behind the wheel, I wanted to squeeze her luscious rump with both hands. God, that creamy skin. Those golden curls! But she'd call the cops. Of course she would. On the other hand, who knows? She's fatherless. World Trade Center.

I creaked upstairs with Chuck panting at my side. He curled up on the window seat and watched as I performed my conjugal duty. I was surprisingly spirited in my thrusts. The champagne, I guess. Afterward I stared at the collision of shadows on the ceiling, waiting for Louise to snore. When I heard nothing, not even breathing, I wondered if she knew how badly I wanted to get downstairs and was torturing me. A car pulled into the driveway. Loud whispers. Laughter. Sarah being dropped off. I thought of our girls and how beautifully Louise had reared them. All the credit goes to her. She is a profoundly generous person. I pulled her onto my chest. I kissed the part in her hair.

"Tonight was fun," I whispered.

"You drank too much," she replied.

I considered telling her that I'd thrown away my anti-depressants three days ago and that this is surely why I'd needed so much booze to feel sane. But I knew what she'd say next, and I didn't want to hear it. What I put into my body is my decision and no one else's. Isn't that what women are always insisting? That's why I'd consulted no one, not even my doctor. Sometimes a person simply has to take control of his own life.

A few minutes later, I slipped out of bed. I came down here to read over my New Year's resolutions from last year, all of which I'd broken by Valentine's Day. Then I chose my best fountain pen and cracked open this leather-bound book, filled with blank pages. My first journal in a quarter

of a century. Much too long. This year my only resolution is
to escape.

◆　◆　◆　◆　◆

Louise reminds me that my fiftieth birthday is approaching
and offers to throw me a birthday party. I tell her no thanks,
dinner with her and the girls is celebration enough. She makes
a pouty face, as though I'd said I intended to spend the night
alone in a tree. Actually, I'm not in the least depressed about
the milestone. Just bewildered. How did I get to be a half
century old? Why do I still look so good? And why, except
for a catalogue of aches and pains, do I feel exactly as I did
at seventeen? Is there no such thing as maturity anymore?
Where are all the grown-ups? When I was a kid, they were
everywhere. Movies were full of them. They wore suits and
ties. Some wore hats. Now all I see are wrinkled adolescents
in T-shirts, sneakers, and jeans, and on weekends I join their
ranks. Louise smiles reassuringly and notes that fifty is the
new forty, but give it some real thought and you realize that
it's actually the new twenty. Dead is the new forty. Tomorrow
I will revise my will, demanding that I be buried in a gray
flannel suit with my face molded into a frown. An adult at last!
Better late than never.

◆　◆　◆　◆　◆

Fred Samuelson wears a bowtie, carries an ivory-handled
walking stick, and smells of citrus aftershave. Although
long retired, he still keeps an office at the accounting firm
he founded four decades years ago. Today on the train,
I mentioned that I was about to turn fifty, and he said that

even though I was still an attractive man, I'd better prepare myself to be ignored by young women. He said at fifty you start to grow dim to them, and by the time you're sixty you're invisible.

"Even if you're rich?" I asked with a twinkle.

"Oh, they might fuck you if you're loaded. Might even marry you. But there's no lust at all. It's not their fault. It's evolutionary. We're on our way out. No one but the undertaker wants to see us naked."

"I guess I'd better be content with my wife, then."

"Or develop a taste for whores."

I would never have expected vulgarity like this from a gentleman so dapper. Sometimes I think that all male decency is either an anomaly or a deception, and that men are, by their very nature, rotten to the core. Consider the reactions I get from other males when I confess that I've never cheated on Louise. With few exceptions, they are bewildered, dismayed, or certain that I am lying.

♦   ♦   ♦   ♦   ♦

Walking through Grand Central, I bade a sad farewell to the colored lights, the public Tchaikovsky, and the subtle cheer on the face of even the most abject commuter. I look forward to the holidays all year, hate them as they're taking place, and miss them the second they're over. My whole life I've struggled to live in the present, but to no avail. Even having kids didn't help. When the girls were toddlers, I imagined delivering them to college, and now that two out of three of them are already there, I grieve the loss of them as toddlers. I would like to think this is because I am a born artist, but it's probably just human.

◆ ◆ ◆ ◆ ◆

A beautiful black woman stood ahead of me in line today at Melody Sandwich. I pictured myself saying hello to her. She flashes a perfect white smile, and after a few minutes, even though she is married, she agrees to join me for a drink at the Algonquin. One Scotch turns into three, and the next thing I know I've booked a room, and we are naked. The sight of our clashing skin colors makes me dizzy with desire. Our coupling is both animal and sacred. Afterward, gulping for air, we agree to meet again next week. The affair refuses to end. Even after I divorce Louise, I do not tell my cocoa paramour that I am single now. I know it will ruin everything.

My reverie abruptly ended when the line moved. The woman stepped to the counter, pointing at a tuna salad on wheat wrapped in plastic. Her head turned profile for a split second and my heart stopped. It was Starla Ferris. I was almost certain of it. And, my God, has she changed. The ghetto girl has grown up! She was poised and womanly, and her taste was impeccable. She wore woolen slacks, elegant brown boots, and a black cashmere coat and scarf. I wanted to say hello to her, but I was afraid.

I fled to Bryant Park and bought a hotdog. What I did to Starla Ferris so many years ago was the low point of my ethical life. Which is why I rarely think of it anymore. But it all returned, and there was nothing I could do to stop it. Sinking onto a bench, I saw the leopard-print panties she wore that afternoon. Her big brown tits overflowing the tight, shiny burgundy bra. The soft steel wool of her groin. I tossed my half-eaten dog into a trashcan and hurried away. My armpits were drenched, and I thought I would vomit. Was it shame or just a result of quitting my meds so abruptly?

♦ ♦ ♦ ♦ ♦

Whenever my powers of analysis fail me, I know that I am
truly alive.

♦ ♦ ♦ ♦ ♦

Chip and Mary Mullins, Bing and Fiona Lang, Bob and Estelle
Platz, came to dinner tonight. Carmen cooked them a succulent
roast beef. Rosa had obviously heeded my threats, because she
served the meal with a minimum of Hispanic chatter and fuss.

Louise was in poor form. Her nervous energy never fails
to pall and exhaust. I always assumed the passage of time
would tire her out, subdue her need to be delightful, and for a
while it looked as though it had, but in the past year her spunk
has rallied to an alarming degree. I think it must be early-
onset menopause. Or perhaps on some unconscious level she
knows what's coming and is terrified of growing old alone.

It is good for me to socialize with other married couples.
Their obvious unhappiness makes me feel better about my
decision to leave. At the same time, I'm grateful that I won't
be gone until September. It will require all of my wisdom and
finesse to exit in just the right way. Not to mention courage.
What's the famous line from *Macbeth?* I must "screw my
courage to the sticking place." Something like that.

♦ ♦ ♦ ♦ ♦

One of the many sacrifices I made to this marriage is that I no
longer have as much poetry committed to memory as I once
did. In Paris, I wrapped Louise in my arms and whispered
Byron in her ear: "And on that cheek, and o'er that brow,
so soft, so calm, yet eloquent...." I was sure she'd swoon.

Instead she crossed her eyes and stuck out her tongue like a mechanical toy. She was only twenty-one, but still.

◆   ◆   ◆   ◆   ◆

I searched Starla Ferris on the computer and found only a few in the entire e-universe. They were all too young, too old, or too white to be mine. And so I returned to the sandwich shop today, hoping to catch another glimpse of her. She did not return, but more memories of her did. Disgraceful ones, because that's all there is.

Back at work, heart still racing, the last person I wanted to see was Juliet Hacker, but there she was, perched on Carole's desk, skirt hiked up, cellulite bared, slurping a giant soda. A human noise machine. Her straw jabbing at her ice was like a rockslide. She honked a big "Hey, boss!" and followed me into my office. She is slovenly, there's no other word for it. Hair greasy, blouse wrinkled, stockings torn, shoes scuffed. And yet the gleam in her eye casts a sensual spell over me. I wish it didn't. Good God, if we ever fucked, imagine the aftermath. Pillow talk with a Canadian goose.

The reason for her visit was a feature she wants to run in the March issue about a social networking site that while boasting just a few thousand members is poised to "kick serious Facebook-ass." I told her as gently as I could that given the state of the world no one cares about this sort of tech startup nonsense anymore. She replied that many people do—they just don't happen to be people my age. I replied that people her age don't buy our magazine, so who cares what interests them? I do, she said, because they love our website, and after the printed version dies, they will make up the core of our paid online subscribers. They will save us!

I am not sure why, but I really let her have it. It went far beyond my own personal dislike of her. (I was destroying an effigy. But of what? What does Juliet represent to me? Ruminate on this.) I told her that print journalists are like dinosaurs, looking up at a sky darkened by volcanic ash and wondering why it's suddenly so nippy out. To believe that our destroyer, the Internet, could save us was sheer lunacy. Did she really think just because the words were sitting on a glowing screen instead of a piece of paper that it would make the least bit of difference to the image-worshiping nitwits of her generation whose disdain for the English language, and thus for organized thought itself, was the most pernicious cultural development since the invention of the nickelodeon?

If I had just left it there, I would be asleep right now instead of fretting, but a young female audience had formed at my door and I wanted to impress them. I pointed a long finger at Juliet and barked that if I heard the words *bemused, nonplussed, disinterested,* and the phrase *beg the question* misused one more time by another one of her generation, I would hold her personally responsible and fire her. "Oh, and one more thing," I said. "Spread the word to your mouse-wielding pals that *feel,* when describing an emotion, is a linking verb that takes an adjective, so that no one feels *badly* except a lout who jams his hand up your shirt and catches his pinkie on your nipple ring!"

Juliet's chin trembled, and she stormed out. Up until then I had thought she was taking it all with a grain of salt. She always acts so tough. I think my audience was as shocked as I was when she wailed "Asshole!" and slammed her door. I wonder if she will quit now. Maybe I did her a favor. She would be so much happier as a blogger. She could stay home all day in sweatpants and wouldn't be required to know much about anything. All you need is opinions. Even dogs have those. They bark at the moon. I sure hope she doesn't tell Doug what happened. Just in case, I'd better start planning my defense.

♦ ♦ ♦ ♦ ♦

Last fall, Louise invited me to join her for a series of lectures on famous local artists, to be conducted over the next three months at the Morrow Estate. When she asked, she was reading in the amber glow of a little mica lamp, and she looked about thirty. I was tempted to say yes, just to make her happy and break up the monotony of winter, but it would have been selfish. After I leave, she will be forced to do things solo. It's better that she gets used to it now. Tonight is the first lecture. She doesn't seem in the least bit depressed to be going alone. Hopeful sign.

♦ ♦ ♦ ♦ ♦

In their spare time, most married men use their computers to watch pornography. I am an exception. Tonight I spent three hours on Google pairing different internal organs with the word *cancer*. My symptoms, which appeared out of nowhere this week, include sharp pains in the area of the ileocecal valve, sporadic head rushes, night sweats, worse than usual prostate pain, and a dramatic tapering of the stool.

The only good thing about hypochondria is that sooner or later (unless I am hit by a moving van) one of my self-diagnoses will be proved correct. One of my false alarms will not be false. When I announce that I am actually dying, everyone who ever laughed at my dire predictions will be silenced and perhaps even a bit ashamed. Could I be on the cusp of it now? Is it my destiny to die, just as my father did, within the shadow of my fiftieth birthday?

♦ ♦ ♦ ♦ ♦

The reason I began taking antidepressants in the first place was to curb obsessional thinking, which the experts say is born of acute anxiety. It's only been eleven days since I flushed my meds down the toilet, but could it be that my obsessions are back already after so many years in abeyance? That I am not dying at all and my symptoms are just figments of an overworked imagination? Or could it be the symptoms are real, but merely the side effects of pharmaceutical withdrawal?

♦ ♦ ♦ ♦ ♦

I emailed Doug today and mentioned my tiff with Juliet Hacker. I haven't heard back from him yet, which is odd, because even though he is in London for the next couple of weeks, he always replies promptly. Equally odd is that no one at work has mentioned the incident. We are a tight-knit group, so at the very least I would have expected some good-natured raillery. When I emailed Doug, it was a mistake to write "Stupid Juliet" on the subject line.

♦ ♦ ♦ ♦ ♦

Waited across the street from Melody Sandwich today. I do not want anything from Starla except to apologize from the bottom of my heart. What happened between us was, after all, a felony in many states. I wonder how much of it she even remembers. I am forever amazed at the capacity of human beings to forget. How sweet it must be to walk through life unburdened by the past. Like bouncing on the moon. If only I had the gift. Before Louise, I slept with twenty-six women. I have relived these sexual encounters so often (usually with Louise snoring next to me) that I can fire off the names of these women in chronological order without a pause. It does not make me happy. I burn with passion and regret.

◆ ◆ ◆ ◆ ◆

Annie flew in for my birthday this afternoon. What a wonderful surprise. Unfortunately, she brought along her new boyfriend. At first I assumed that my almost instant dislike of Joshua Mendel was simple jealousy, the natural antipathy of a father toward his usurper. But now I am think my dislike of the kid is based solely on the fact that he is objectively loathsome and repulsive.

On the most superficial level, he has the sort of craggy horse face that on a Celt is considered ugly, but on a Jew is considered sexy. Or maybe it's the other way around. Who cares? Forget his face. He is an egotistical creep. Five times in the first twenty minutes he referred to himself as a "filmmaker." I wouldn't have minded it so much if he hadn't shot only one film in his life and it's eight minutes long and silent. Turns out Joshua is a twenty-seven-year-old sophomore at a third-rate film school. I guess calling himself a filmmaker is the sort of hubris one ought to expect from a kid who wears a Cubs cap indoors when meeting his girlfriend's parents for the first time. When we sat down to eat, he finally took it off, revealing a shredded hairline. I burst out laughing. No one knew why.

Because Joshua likes to eat even more than he likes to

talk about himself, dinner was fairly pleasurable. The girls, as usual, picked up right where they had left off. Karen, a budding lesbian, is becoming more and more politically radical by the minute, i.e., simple-minded and rigid in regard to the world's most intractable problems. Sarah, much prettier, eschews politics altogether and wishes everyone would just chill out and be happy. As the two sparred, Annie, the aspiring attorney, mediated with insight and good humor.

Sadly, Louise was in another of her loud, loopy moods. When I blew out my candles a bit too hastily for her tastes, she cried out: "Baby, you didn't make a wish! Or did you? Did you make a wish? What did you wish for?"

"More coffee," I said, holding up my cup to Rosa.

"Oh, Mal," Louise tsked.

"What? I like to set my sights low. That way I'm never disappointed."

Annie shot me a stern look, as though she knew I was referring in the most oblique way to my marriage.

After I had opened my presents, Karen and Sarah toasted me with sincere affection, Louise with frantic hyperbole, and Annie with lyrical sadness, reminding us all that little Archer would have turned sixteen last month. While it's vital that we don't forget him, uttering his name shatters Louise in a way that Annie can't possibly imagine, ignorant as she is of her mother's role in his death. Everyone got misty-eyed but me. But even if I had felt like crying, I would have resisted, simply because there was a stranger present—one who chews with his mouth open.

After dinner, I took Chuck for a slow walk by the river, during which I cadged a much needed smoke from a passing stranger. The world was frozen and crouched, waiting for something to happen. It began to snow. Once New Year's has passed, snow is just a dirty inconvenience. When I got back to my study, I poured myself a stiff drink and started a fire. As I reached for my journal, the phone rang. Louise calling from upstairs, asking how I felt about Annie and Josh sharing a bed under our roof. Even though the idea sickens me, I said, "Fine by me." To have answered any other way would have broken the first rule of parenting: Never try to control the sexual behavior of a child over thirteen, unless you want the behavior to become chronic.

◆　◆　◆　◆　◆

When a knock at the door disturbed my last entry, I stashed the journal and raised the volume on the TV, which I always leave on as a precaution. Annie's brow twitched when she entered and saw what I was watching.

"You like this?"

I looked at the TV. One of those real-life prison shows, where muscle-bound, tattooed sociopaths discuss everything under the sun.

"Who doesn't? It's real."

She settled by the fire with Chuck. She wore nothing but boxers, a T-shirt, and pink, fuzzy slippers. Such a gorgeous girl. From me she got her pale skin, fine cheekbones, black eyes, straight nose, broad shoulders, and good height. Louise contributed the freckles, dimples, and knock-knees.

At first, she said nothing, petting Chuck and gazing through leaded-glass at the softly falling snow. She asked when I was going to finally tear down the jungle gym. I told her soon, and we both knew it was unlikely. She smiled and began to talk about her new man. How he is a lovable lunatic who eats, drinks, and sleeps film.

"Does he shit it, too?"

"Be nice," she laughed.

"You can't make me. It's my birthday."

"You already got your present."

"Then take it back."

"You don't like it?"

"Are you kidding? Who doesn't want a biography of Truman? I love it. I want to be buried with it."

"Why are you being so aggressive?"

"Because I'm dying. I'm fifty now. It's just a matter of time, you know."

She grinned. "What do you think it'll be? Pancreatic?"

"Bile duct."

"How come?"

"It's rare and fast. It just feels right."

We both laughed. No one on earth understands me as well as she does. Maybe that's why her face looked so anxious when she resumed.

"Look, I know it's easy to joke about Joshua and his filmmaking, because he's young and just starting out, but trust me, it's what he was born to do. I know because he's tried to quit and can't. It's his destiny. A blessing and a curse."

"Deuteronomy me no Deuteronomy."

"Huh?"

"Every young artist says he'd die if he was forced to quit, but most do quit, and they don't die. In fact, they're better off for it. So is the world."

"God, you're harsh."

"I'm just telling you the truth as I know it."

"You and Joshua are different. It was easy for you to quit writing, because you were never really a writer in the first place. You're a born editor. I mean, obviously. Look at how successful you've been. But Joshua's wanted to make movies since he was, like, five years old." She exhaled heavily. Time to break the news. "Anyway, he's made a huge decision. He's dropping out of school. He's going to use his tuition money to finance a short film. Something he can enter into contests and use as a calling card."

I managed a smile. "What's it about?"

"A retired butcher named Stanley Fisch. His only dream since he was a little boy is to go over Niagara Falls in a barrel. One day he quits his job, buys a bathing suit and an old wine cask. Everyone tells him he's insane, but he doesn't listen. He drives north and goes over the falls. The barrel bounces and bounces all the way down, but at the bottom it's totally undamaged. A miracle. The cops open it and there's nothing inside. No Stanley Fisch. It's all about how once your dreams come true, existence is no longer necessary."

"It's called 'Fisch in a Barrel.'"

Her mouth fell open. "How did you know that?"

"I'm a born editor."

"What do you think?"

The truth was painful to admit. "It's original and smart."

"I know, right?"

"It could be a gem. But if he screws it up even a little bit—"

"I'm not worried. He'll do an amazing job. It starts shooting in June. He wants me to produce it for him."

"What do you know about producing?"

"Nothing. I'll learn."

"But I thought you committed to Bates, Whitson."

"I'll be a summer associate *next* year. This is much more important."

I sucked a deep breath. My mind churned with invective. I leaned down, took her hand in mine, and spoke from the heart: "Sweetheart, you have a dazzling life ahead of you. There's nothing in the world you can't be or do or have, if you set your mind to it. To defer your own dreams, even for one second, for the sake of this guy would be the worst mistake. He's mediocre. He'll drag you down with him." Pretty measured, all things considered. Of course Annie did not agree. Her face hardened. She rose and left without so much as a good night.

I feel rotten about it now. I broke my own rule. She'll probably marry the toad now. Anyway, she had it coming. Insulting me on my birthday. A born editor! Fuck that. Boy, is she in for a surprise. Time to down a fistful of antacids and go to sleep. Up, dear Chuck, let us leave this day to its sorry end. If Annie hates me now, imagine how she will feel after I divorce her mother. She'll never speak to me again. I can't imagine anything worse. Except, perhaps, cancer of the asshole.

◆　◆　◆　◆　◆

Winter is sinking its teeth into the city like a bear trap. Fierce headache this morning. I'm still shitting ribbons. One more week of this and I will call a doctor.

◆　◆　◆　◆　◆

Ellie Gardner, seven months pregnant, is a teacher of sixth-grade English. Her husband, Greg, is a real estate broker. Although one might imagine that the blue-blooded Louise would have little in common with two such red-blooded Americans, it turns out they share a love of necrophilic cultural cannibalism. For the past three Wednesdays, they have sat together at the Morrow Estate, watching an expert pick clean the bones of dead artists. Then they regroup at a local chain restaurant to relive the highlights: Kurt Weill's father was a cantor. Carson McCullers's real name was Lulu Smith. Edward Hopper had a bum prostate. (No wonder!) Louise came home tonight like a schoolgirl with a crush, gushing about what great fun she had with her new pals. I say all the right things, but there's one thing she'll never hear me say: "So when do *I* get to meet them?"

◆ ◆ ◆ ◆ ◆

Doug Viertel was finally back at work today. I greeted him as warmly as I always do, hoping that he would stop and shoot the breeze with me. I even had a joke all planned out: "Hey, what happened between Juliet and me? The fault isn't in ourselves. It's in the stars. We have conflicting zodiac signs. I'm stubborn as a bull and she has crabs." But before I could get two words out, he walked right past me. The snub was witnessed by Tammy from accounting, who looked away, mortified, waiting for me to disappear. I am still reeling from the blow.

◆ ◆ ◆ ◆ ◆

It's incredible how memories can rise from the dead. I must set them down here, so that if I ever decide to write a short story about Starla Ferris, I will have them at my fingertips.

At the time Starla and I met, I was working as a maid for an elderly agoraphobic millionaire. Because I worked for him six days a week from 5 until 9 a.m. and because I cleaned every room in his townhouse except for the one in which he slept until 10 a.m., I never actually met the beast, although I did launder his huge underwear and polish the silver frame that held his monstrous photographic portrait. His standards of hygiene were so strict that it was not unusual for me to clean a room knowing that it had not been stepped foot in since I'd scoured it the morning before. Sisyphus with a toilet brush. Yet I was unbowed. Quite the opposite, walking to work in the wintry darkness, I would be overwhelmed by the certainty that my suffering was part of a master plan, the dues required of the brilliant literary career that awaited me. It was all I could do to stifle a scream of joy and anticipation.

Around this time, there was deafening construction going on next door to my tenement apartment building, so I wrote each day at the 42nd Street library. Although there were branches much closer, many famous authors had worked at this one, and I wanted to carry on the tradition. So every morning, still reeking of bleach and ammonia, I hunkered down over a legal pad in the Main Reading Room and scratched away with an antique fountain pen. I even brought along an inkwell. Hard to believe but true. Every young artist is ridiculous in his own way.

Unfortunately, I got no more accomplished in the hallowed silence of the library than I would have at home with my thumbs in my ears. Oh, I toiled all right, filling page after page, but every evening on my way out, I dropped them into the trash. My problem was simple: I was young and serious, and while frivolous work comes easily at any age, serious work is never harder than when one is ignorant on a wide array of subjects and has nothing original to say.

When I wasn't actually writing, I was daydreaming. My most cherished fantasy was that at any moment a gorgeous young female novelist, preferably from England or Ireland, would sit down next to me with a legal pad of her own. We would break out laughing at the coincidence, and our fates would be sealed. We would spend the rest of our lives together, writing great books side by side. At night, we'd read Victorian novels before the crackling fire while our angelic children played quietly on the carpet.

Instead, I looked up one day and there, sitting across from me, was an actual human being. Ilene Goss was her name, a modern dancer, killing time between rehearsals. Among her many virtues was that she had decided within minutes of meeting me that we were soul mates. I did not feel the same way, but I was flattered and did not want to disappoint her.

After a delirious first month in bed, I began to notice a few troubling things. A steady drizzle of despair fell in her eyes, even when she smiled. Her East Village apartment was a study in self-loathing: dirty dishes piled high, newspapers and magazines littering the floors, and, at the foot of her closet, a heap of dirty leotards on which five cats slept. All of this, combined with illegible handwriting, rust-stained toilet, untweezed nipple hair, and doting daddy who paid her rent, suggested to me that Ilene was emotionally stunted and that her declarations of undying love were not to be trusted. Yet trust them I did. I banished my premonitions and gave her what she had been begging for in word and deed almost since the moment we met: surrender. I told her that I loved her, too.

The very next night when I knocked on her door to take her to dinner, there was no answer. I called her from the pay phone downstairs, and when she finally picked up she was sobbing her guts out. I assumed that a family member had died, or, at the very least, one of her cats. She said she didn't know what was happening to her but that she couldn't stop crying and that I should just go home. I ran back upstairs,

banged on her door, talked my way in, and held her in my arms
as she wept. I pinched a tissue to her nose and assured her that
what was happening to her was perfectly natural. I had fallen
in love with her, and now that she had gotten what she wanted,
she was scared to death. She was terrified of commitment.
Everyone was. She smiled, sniffled, and led me to her bed.

"Never give up on me," she whispered.

"I won't," I vowed.

When I knocked on her door two nights later, she was
sobbing again, but this time I couldn't talk my way in. In fact,
the longer I pleaded with her to open up, the more violently
she wept. She said that she had never loved me and that
she'd told me we were soul mates because she thought I was
insecure and needed to hear it. She said that if I really loved
her as much as I claimed, I would leave and never come back. I
screamed at her (something terrible about how she would die
alone and be eaten by her cats) and stormed away.

The next few months were among the most painful of my
young life. I was poisoned with rage, not only at Ilene but at
all women. I wore my misogyny on my sleeve. Deprived of
the civilizing effect of females, I regressed to the cave. I did
not regularly shower or shave. I smoked in crowded elevators
and spat in empty ones. I read nothing but Nietzsche and
Schopenhauer, vowing never to trust again.

One day, quite by accident, I picked up a magazine
called *Chocolate Kisses*, filled with personal ads. You could
place or answer a listing the traditional way, by letter, or else
take advantage of the magazine's state-of-the-art voicemail
system. I had never dated a black woman, but I figured it
was worth a try. Who knows, I might discover that it wasn't
women who were rotten to the core, just *white* women. My
ad went something like this: "Tall, fit, attractive, idealistic

white writer, 24, seeks gorgeous, intelligent black woman, 20-30, for romance and adventure. I will rock you all night long, girl." Looking back, I am not surprised that my funky farewell repelled precisely the sort of female I wanted to attract and filled my voice mailbox with greetings from freaks. A male teenager shouted "Faggot!" A baritone transsexual asked me to describe my "gentles." A Latina cab driver with three kids said she wanted to be "real honest about her herbies." God, people are stupid. Just as I had given up hope, I received a message from a female who said she liked my ad and would be "most honored" if I called her back.

Starla Ferris answered on the first ring. Her voice was like a rich, warm syrup. She confessed right off the bat that she was younger than what I was looking for. Only nineteen. She asked if this was a problem. I said that in terms of building a long-term relationship, yes, it was a major problem, but for a romantic adventure, it was no problem at all. She said an adventure was what she wanted, too, because she and her boyfriend, Ashmore, had just broken up after two years, and she just wanted to have fun right now.

"Well, you've come to the right place," I said.

◆ ◆ ◆ ◆ ◆

Read some Updike today. I know I am in the minority, but I find him a deadly bore.

◆ ◆ ◆ ◆ ◆

Dinner at Teddy and Meg's new house. It's a hovel compared to their old place. An underreported pleasure of economic downturns is that so many people who deserve to suffer do.

I mean, honestly, who deserves to suffer more than Teddy? Hoping to recoup more of his lost fortune, he kept probing to see if I had any insider secrets. I assured him, as I do everyone who probes, that I have no interest in Wall Street and that the only reason I've worked so long at a business magazine is that I enjoy making bad writing good. I would be just as happy (or unhappy) working for a bodybuilding magazine, or one of those rags for mercenaries and gun nuts. Whenever I say this, people burst out laughing as though I'd just performed a terrific card trick, but I really mean it.

◆　◆　◆　◆　◆

Doug Viertel's first order of business today was to call me into his office. When I got there, Betsy Paul (Director of Human Resources) was already sitting on the couch, legs crossed, smirking. It could mean only one thing: I was about to get fired. For the fun of it, I spent the next ten minutes making banal small talk, not to stall the inevitable but simply to make them squirm. And did they ever! I wish I had it on tape, because it was funny. Every time there was a pause and Doug cleared his throat to get down to business, I would chime in with another idiotic observation. Banal conventional wisdom, delivered as though it were profound.

When Doug couldn't bear it another moment, he interrupted with force. He said that it was time for me and the company to part ways and that he was offering me early retirement. I was genuinely surprised and confused. Was I being pushed out because I had thrashed Juliet or because I was old? I had assumed the former. I could accept the former. I sat back and asked if this offer was specific to me or part of a company-wide initiative targeting older editors.

"It's specific to you. I'm offering you a chance to exit with dignity. If that interests you."

"Why wouldn't it?"

"The way you've been behaving lately," Betsy interjected, "I'd say dignity is pretty low on your list of priorities."

I matched her snotty tone. "And how have I been behaving, Ms. Paul?"

Doug asked: "Just what exactly gave you the idea it was okay to tear Juliet's head off just because she pitched you a story you didn't like?"

"I didn't tear her head off. I yelled at it."

I expected him to smile, but he was in no mood. I looked over at Betsy and neither was she. I casually crossed my legs at the knee, like a languid aristocrat, and explained that my harangue had been entirely tongue-in-cheek. I and everyone else thought that Juliet was enjoying the joke as much as we were. It was only when she stormed off in a huff that we realized her feelings had been hurt.

"I felt sick about it," I concluded. "Just sick."

"Then why didn't you apologize?" Betsy asked.

"What?"

"You heard me."

Doug took over: "You didn't apologize because there was nothing playful about it. It was abusive. Everyone who witnessed it was appalled. You even scared Carol. She was afraid you were going to hit her."

"Oh, please. Why would I hit Carol? I like her. It's Juliet I can't stand."

Betsy talked slowly, as though to an imbecile: "It was *Juliet* she was afraid you were going to hit."

"Oh. Okay."

"Leaving aside the cruelty of your attack," Doug continued, "the actual content of what you asserted—"

"Please don't get me started. I could write a book about it."

"—is inane. Are you aware that the only thing keeping us afloat these days is the revenue stream from our website? A full thirty-eight percent of our advertising revenue comes from online ads."

"I was not aware of that," I said.

Doug glanced at Betsy. She opened a folder. The pleasantries were over. She proceeded to recite every single complaint lodged against me in the past three years—most of them niggling to the point of absurdity. At last she reached her conclusion: "They demonstrate a pattern of misconduct that suggests a willful and deepening disregard for the rules of appropriate conduct."

I burst out laughing. I couldn't help it. What a load of shit.

Betsy's eyes flared darkly. "Your relationship with the company ends today. It can happen in one of two ways. Retirement or termination. Your choice."

She explained that if I retired, I would receive an exit bonus of $1,000 per year of service and would maintain full control over my pension. But if I was terminated—

"Hold it right there, honey," I said. "Where do I sign?"

Doug and Betsy were stunned. They had expected if not mortal combat then at the very least a nasty tussle. Doug slid a document toward me. I picked it up and skimmed it. The usual boilerplate. Just as I was about to touch pen to paper, I looked up at Doug and saw fear in his eye. I realized that I could ask for just about anything right now and I'd get it.

"One condition," I said, lifting the golden tip and creaking back in my chair. "Or else I'll fight you. I shall fight you on the beaches, I shall fight you on the landing grounds, I shall fight you in the fields and in the streets."

"What do you want?" Doug sighed.

"Discretion. No farewell party. No announcement in the newsletter. Keep my email and voicemail active until September. If anyone asks, I'm on special assignment." I pointed at him. "And not a word to your blabbermouth wife."

"What's Iris got to do with it?"

"She and Louise lunch occasionally. I want to keep this from Louise for as long as possible."

He stared as though I were nuts, then he smiled and agreed. With a few flicks of my wrist, I was unemployed. No longer an editor, born or otherwise.

◆　◆　◆　◆　◆

A white rat every morning at the sound of a bell shoots into a bare corridor of sharp turns. Nose twitching, it scampers left, right, left, left, left, until, there at last, it faces its golden cheesy reward. This has been my life for the past twenty-four years, three months, and two days. My only relief from the deadly routine has been Augusts in Nantucket, which, with its cocktail parties and clambakes, is a different sort of maze, offering not cheddar but a wedge of Brie. I hate Brie. Brie smells foul when it's fresh; imagine it after it's spent a day or two in your guts. But I digress. Where was I? Oh, yes, nowhere. What a magnificent place to be. Tomorrow is Monday, and I have nothing to do. No plans or commitments of any kind. In many ways it's providential. I have time to get my affairs in order well before Karen starts college, and I begin my new life.

◆　◆　◆　◆　◆

Blue skies, brisk wind. I walked all the way from Grand Central to the Reservoir, then turned around and made it back in time for lunch hour outside Melody Sandwich. I bought a pack of organic cigarettes and smoked three as I lingered. They tasted great, and for the first time in years I did not feel ashamed of my lust for nicotine. Maybe it's best that Starla not return. I do not need the distraction of nostalgia right now. Or even of repentance.

I hopped a bus to the Strand, where I bought a few used books, not the sort a magazine editor buys to kill a commute, but the kind an artist buys to enliven his imagination. I walked west to Emile's. I first gave up the artist's life while visiting Paris, so what better place to celebrate its recapture than a French bistro, reading Paul Verlaine's *Confessions* over steak frites and a bottle of humble red? As hard as it is to admit, Juliet Hacker gave me the gift that I was unwilling to give myself. If I run into her, I will not punch her in the mouth as I had planned. I will kiss her instead. On both cheeks. Liberté!

◆ ◆ ◆ ◆ ◆

Whither Wander? An excellent title for a novel about a middle-aged banker who is fired from his job and spends his days wandering Manhattan, seeking a purpose. Or is it too old-fashioned? When is old-fashioned going to make a comeback? What if I have been away from the literary scene for so long that I have nothing to say to young readers? I need a story that I am burning to tell. I will return to the 42nd Street library for inspiration.

◆ ◆ ◆ ◆ ◆

When I got home tonight, red-cheeked, happy, and lying through my teeth about the sloppy work of one of our new freelancers, Louise said, "What's going on?"

My heart stopped. "Come again?"

"If I didn't know better, I'd think you were having an affair."

I hid my relief. "What do you mean 'know better'? You insult me. Why *couldn't* I be having an affair?"

"Because you love me too much."

I must have smiled a bit too convincingly, because she threw her arms around my neck, pressed her wrinkled freckles to my face, and tried to pull me down onto the couch. I laughed it off and said that I needed some time to decompress, and, besides, what if Karen walked in?

Ten minutes later, Karen did walk in, unexpectedly, which made me feel less guilty about rejecting my wife.

"See?" I whispered.

Louise laughed. "Like you would have lasted this long."

Was she flattering herself or insulting me again?

Fact is, I do finish quickly most of the time, but only because we rarely have sex, and because most of the time I have a nagging feeling that she is only vaguely enjoying herself. Many men would resent this lack of passion and use it as an excuse to stray. But I never have.

Today a fresh-faced, curvy Russian girl, no older than twenty-five, struck up a conversation with me outside Melody Sandwich. Before she sashayed off, she insisted that I take her phone number and email address. At first I was pleased with myself, but then I remembered what Fred Samuelson said about men as they grow older. Was this girl a prostitute? Not an altogether unappealing thought. I would rather fuck a prostitute than carry on a love affair. The former is to make a mistake that memory can erase; the latter is to live every moment as a fugitive. And yet when I imagine paying for sex, I feel a stabbing pain deep in my prostate, as though I had sat on a knitting needle.

Speaking of health, I have been loosed from the shackles of daily employment for a mere three days, and already my bowels have returned to normal, my stomach pains have eased, and my night sweats have passed. Sadly, my prostate is worse than ever. It must be because, in terms of opportunity, nothing would be easier right now than for me to find sex outside my marriage.

♦ ♦ ♦ ♦ ♦

As long as a football field, with gorgeous arched windows and eighteen chandeliers running down its length, the Main Reading Room of the 42nd Street library is a municipal treasure. It is resplendent in its beauty and timeless in its charm. Yet it is open to everyone, even the homeless. The price of admission is curiosity. The chair is comfy. Overhead, painted clouds. What a glorious place to create.

In artistic terms, I have squandered my life. The test of my maturity will be the degree to which I can atone for it with a third act of sustained creation. Setting down what happened between Starla and me has done wonders for my self-confidence, because I believe it contains the finest prose I have spun since my bachelor days. Whether I have it in me to write something more substantial remains to be seen. First I need a story. The world is filled with writers who prattle on and on without ever getting to *Once upon a time*. They are essayists in disguise. The last thing the world needs is another Philip Roth whose stories are simply camouflage for righteous lectures. Everything I have to say must be embedded in a beginning, middle, and an end. Something to keep the tribe engrossed around the campfire at night. And yet the narrative must be vast enough to reflect the full scope of my aspirations.

◆ ◆ ◆ ◆ ◆

The next afternoon I waited for Starla on my front stoop, sitting next to Elliot Raskin, my upstairs neighbor, a gay travel agent from Queens with a hunchback and a giant toupee. (Although it resembled a raccoon standing on its hind legs, he boasted that it was undetectable.) Elliot's sex life was so sordid that I knew he would never pass judgment on mine, and so I filled him in on my blind date. Delighted by the intrigue, he lit one of his skinny brown cigarettes and asked what Starla looked like. When I realized that I had never asked for a photograph, I panicked. She had told me that she was "super-sexy," but so what? Ilene Goss had said she loved me. What had I gotten myself into? I was about to be creamed again.

"Look," I said, "I have no idea what she looks like. Or even who she is. She's already twenty minutes late. For all I know, she could be a drag queen with a knife."

"That would be a bad thing?"

"Be serious. I need your help. Will you help me?"

He shrugged his shoulders. "Sure, I got nothin' to do."

"Okay, here's the plan. When her cab pulls up, you and I will get up and walk down the block. When she gets out of the car, I'll turn around and look at her. If she's pretty, I'll walk back and greet her, and you go on your merry way, but if she's ugly or in any way freakish, we'll keep walking. When she calls to ask where I was, I'll just say I left because she was late, and I find tardiness unforgivable."

He flicked an ash. "Love it."

A few minutes later, a taxi turned the corner and roared toward us. Without a word, we rose and walked. Elliot hooked his arm in mine and laid his wig on my shoulder. I did not even glance at the cab as it sped past. When I heard the car door slam, I glanced over my shoulder, and there, looking up at my building, was an adorable milk-chocolate bombshell no taller than five foot two with a big bust, bright crimson lips, and a tiny waist pinched by a black patent-leather belt. I slapped Elliot on the hump and dashed off.

As we walked up the five flights to my hovel, I told Starla that she was beautiful, and she said that I was, too. As I was about to unlock the door, she handed me an envelope. Inside was a card in which she had written, next to a lipstick kiss, "Let's fool around!" I kissed her deeply on the mouth right there. Then, to the sound of the workmen's hammers, I proceeded to kiss her all the way through the living room to my bed.

She smelled of spearmint gum. Her skin was preternaturally smooth. I unbuttoned her shirt and unhooked her burgundy bra, freeing her enormous breasts. She unzipped my jeans. I rubbed the silky leopard print that barely covered her damp mound. But then, as she grabbed my cock, a sudden realization jolted me alert. On the phone she had said that she and Ashmore had recently broken up after two years together, but upon entering my apartment I had muttered how good it was to kiss her after not having kissed anyone in ages, and she had replied, "Me too. I've been with the same boy since I was thirteen."

My eyes opened wide. "Starla, you're fifteen."

She grabbed my face with both hands. "Don't be mad! Please don't be mad!"

"I'm not, but—"

"You are!" She kissed me desperately, over and over again. "I was afraid to tell you!"

She began to tug my cock, guiding it towards her open legs. I resisted, breathing hard, unable to decide what to do. To make love to her would be a crime in the eyes of Man, but to walk away a crime in the eyes of men. In the end I took the high moral ground. Unfortunately, in order to reach it, I had to crawl over her face.

What haunts me today as I wait for her outside Melody Sandwich is not the sex act itself. It's what happened later, after I had dismounted, when I reached for the box of tissues to wipe off her chin and neck. She whispered, "That's right, clean up your baby."

◆ ◆ ◆ ◆ ◆

With so much sudden free time, I am able to attend to various errands that I have been putting off, such as having my teeth cleaned. As much as I like Dr. Robbins, I couldn't call her, because if I had, in order to maintain the illusion that I still work at the magazine, I would have been forced to take my usual time slot and waste a perfectly good Saturday afternoon. And so I have found a new dentist, someone with an office in the city who can see me on a weekday. Just for the fun of it, I gave his girl a fake name and told her I would pay in cash.

◆ ◆ ◆ ◆ ◆

Instead of immersing myself in all the works of a single great author, as I did in my youth, I will gather around me a variety of books and delve into each only until my interest flags. Then

I will move on to the next. This way my imagination will be teased, wooed, and stoked but never dominated. If I am going to develop my own style, I must be wary of influences.

◆ ◆ ◆ ◆ ◆

George Meredith: "The most dire disaster in love is the death of the imagination." I tend to agree with this, which is why an artist must be so careful when it comes to marriage.

◆ ◆ ◆ ◆ ◆

My new dentist, Dr. Mort Halperin, has beady eyes, a sour smell, and black-pepper pores in his nose, but he has an air of stone-faced professionalism that inspires immediate trust. After poking around in my mouth for less than a minute, he said that I needed a night guard.

"Why? I stopped grinding my teeth years ago."

"You get headaches?

"Sure, who doesn't?"

"Open wide."

I did, and there was a popping sound.

"Hear that? You need a guard. You also need a cleaning. You know what deep scaling is?"

"Yeah, it's painful. Do you offer gas?"

"Seventy-five bucks extra."

"Let's do it."

A pretty Puerto Rican oral hygienist with penciled-on eyebrows wheeled in the tank. As she set it up, she seemed not to have the faintest idea what she was doing, but I was far too excited to care. Nitrous oxide is about as close to enlightenment as I get. Under its influence, all my worries melt away and the mysteries of the universe are unlocked. Ten seconds after I wake up, I forget it all, but so what?

She slipped the rubber cup over my nose and turned the valve. I heard the hiss and, a few moments later, smelled the menthol. I inhaled with gusto, like a pimply-faced teen into a bag of glue. I noticed for the first time that there was music playing from the sound system. A castrati band from the 1970s. America, I think. Growing woozy, I murmured, "Prepare for lift-off," and she laughed.

Shit. Louise is calling me to dinner. I smell cabbage. If I don't hurry up, she will start clattering the dinner bell and yelling "Come and get it! Come and get it!" and I will want to shoot myself. I will finish my incredible tale later.

◆ ◆ ◆ ◆ ◆

When the nitrous oxide first kicked in, I was all smiles, bodysurfing on a wave that I prayed would never break. Then I fell asleep, sinking into the depths of my unconscious. When I woke up, I was kneeling naked before a towering alien creature, half-insect, half-reptile, and perhaps thirty feet tall. It had traveled millions of light-years to take control of all human thought. My brain was the last one offering any resistance, but I knew I couldn't hold out much longer. When I surrendered at last, it would mean the end of consciousness as we knew it. Mankind would be enslaved forever.

Then, suddenly, I was speeding through white clouds into outer space, moving like a rocket, my whole body shaking. I was conscious enough to think: "This is not a dream! This is real!" Through the clouds, a face appeared. A little boy smiled and blinked at me. I laughed to myself. He reminded me of Archer.

I opened my eyes and discovered that I was now in a cold, white hospital room. A blond nurse entered. She looked down at me, shook her head, and spoke with warmth.

"It's a shame you're dying. You would have grown up to be such a beautiful young man."

"Really?" I said. "How old am I?"

"Six."

I was stunned that I was so young, and then I thought, "What a weird coincidence. Archer died when he was six."

What made all of this nonsense so troubling was that it did not feel like nonsense. It was as real as that clock ticking on my mantel or the fire crackling in my hearth. No, even more real than that. As real as dear old Chuck snoring at my slippers.

Abruptly I was waking up. "Horse with No Name" was playing on the sound system, and it was the scariest thing I had ever heard in my life. When I opened my eyes, Dr. Halperin was shaking me by the shoulders and shouting my name. Once I had gathered my wits, he apologized and told me that Alma, his hygienist, had accidentally given me too much gas. Rattled, he hurried out of the room.

I stood up to go and almost toppled. I was dizzy, weak in the knees, and terribly nauseated. Alma caught me by the elbow and forced me to drink water. Her hands were trembling and her face was slick with sweat. She said that during the deep scaling I was fine. It wasn't until later, when they were measuring me for my night guard, that I had started to moan. As they shook me, I continued moaning, saying goodbye to someone over and over again. I never said a name. I presume it was Louise. But might it have been Archer? What did he have to do with any of this? He has been dead for so many years.

◆   ◆   ◆   ◆   ◆

When I awoke this morning, Louise handed me the phone and told me to call in sick. She said I looked pale as death. I dialed the office and a recorded voice told me that my extension had been disconnected. So much for Doug and Betsy keeping their word. They're worse than shit. Good thing almost everyone reaches me on my cell. For the benefit of Louise, I told the outgoing voice that I was sick as a dog and would not be coming in. I rolled onto my stomach and did not move a muscle all day. What has this dentist done to me?

◆ ◆ ◆ ◆ ◆

Karen confessed tonight that she's worried about me. She says I seem totally up and down lately, but that even when I seem really up, I seem sort of down. Even though what she said was barely English (and yet, compared to her classmates, she is Demosthenes), I knew what she meant. Living a lie creates a subtext of melancholy that cannot be entirely hidden except by sociopaths. I did not confess to anything, of course. I just said that I was touched by her concern but was absolutely fine. Really. Just worn down by the holidays. A touch of the flu.

I think that of my three girls, Karen, although the least flexible, is the one most likely to forgive me for breaking up the family. As an emerging lesbian, she is an outsider like me, a tortured soul who understands the complexity of the human condition.

I will never get used to my children worrying about me. I spent so many years worrying about them. After Annie was born, I would lie in bed at night, thinking of her little heart pounding away in her crib, and I would have to stop myself from crying out in sheer terror at all the things that might harm or kill her. The only thing more courageous than being alive is bringing another being into the world and sentencing them to the same fate.

♦ ♦ ♦ ♦ ♦

This morning Louise announced that we were having dinner with pregnant Ellie Gardner and her husband Greg—not because she thought it would be fun for me, or even for them, but because Ellie needed my help with something. I admit this caught my attention. What could I do for a total stranger? Louise explained that Ellie believes it's a husband's duty to make love to his pregnant wife right up until the moment of delivery. Greg obviously disagrees, because he hasn't laid a hand on her in months. It's breaking her heart. Too humiliated to ask him why, Ellie wants me to do it for her.

"But I don't even know the guy."

"That's the whole point. Ellie says Greg's intensely private, and his friends know it. Only a stranger would have the gall to ask him about something so personal."

Even though I had promised myself that I would steer clear of the Gardners, I saw how badly Louise wanted to come through for her pal. When a tiny gesture can bring a loved one so much happiness, it's mean spirited to refuse.

When we arrived at Brighella, the Gardners were already waiting at a table for four, wearing identical smiles and munching breadsticks. Greg is vapid, overfriendly, and incapable of an original thought. So is Ellie, but she more than makes up for it by being cute as a button. Shiny, short black hair. Pale skin. Deep blue eyes. Bright white smile. As she struggled to her feet to shake my hand, I stepped back in shock. Her tits lay sprawled like seal pups across her enormous belly. Her biceps were mannish and her legs were as shapely as barber poles. Only her pretty little wrists hinted at the girl she had once been, before Greg dumped his seed in her.

During dinner, I learned that what the Gardners and Louise love most about the Morrow lectures is the over-arching message they convey, which is that geniuses are flesh and blood just like you and me. In fact, some of them were actually our neighbors, and a few even rot in our local cemeteries. Implicit in all this is that anyone can be a genius. All you have to do is haul the easel down from the attic, tune that old piano, or audition to play Annie Oakley at the Hudson Valley Playhouse.

"When I met Mal, he was an aspiring novelist," Louise offered.

"No kidding," Greg said.

"What happened?" Ellie asked, eyes widening, as though we were at the climax of a murder mystery.

"Her old man bribed me to quit," I said.

The Gardners laughed.

Louise smiled uneasily. "Well, that's not quite accurate."

"Sure it is," I said, twirling my linguine. "It was either the smartest thing I ever did or the stupidest. Who knows what I might have accomplished if I'd told him to go to hell?"

"My father never told him to stop writing. He just wanted him to bring home a paycheck. Lots of writers work nine-to-five jobs."

"William Carlos Williams was a doctor," Greg said.

"T. S. Eliot was a bank clerk," Ellie said.

"Wallace Stevens sold insurance," Louise added.

I felt like screaming: "How the fuck do you philistines know so much?" Instead I held it together and said, "Yeah, I guess I could have come home from work every night and started writing, but I chose to hang out with my kids instead.

Teach them to read. Help them with their homework. Tuck them in. Maybe I wasn't self-centered enough."

"Don't listen to him," Louise said. "He's plenty self-centered."

Everyone laughed but me.

"Well, maybe someday when you retire," Greg said, "you can take another stab at it. Sure beats golf."

"Great American Novel, here you come!" Ellie chortled, lifting her water glass.

They all toasted.

As soon as the plates were cleared, Louise and Ellie excused themselves so that I could begin my probe. I was in a foul mood now, and since I had no stake in the outcome, I dispensed with any semblance of tact.

"Greg, are you one of those guys who likes to screw right up until the baby's crowning, or are you more like me, a guy who holsters his cock around month three?"

He jerked back in his seat as though I had spit in his eye, then, once he had recovered from the shock, he leaned forward and answered eagerly. He is not a private person at all. He couldn't wait to unload.

"I'm crazy about Ellie," he whispered, "but from the minute she told me she was pregnant, sex was the last thing I wanted. I faked it for a while, but once she started showing, there was no way I could get it up. Why does everyone say pregnant women are beautiful? They're not!"

"Everyone doesn't say it. Women say it. Just waiting for a guy to disagree. But we don't. Because we're afraid. Very afraid."

Greg smiled, relieved to be understood.

Just for the fun of it, I added: "What about oral? You ever give Ellie oral just to make her feel wanted?"

His eyes bulged with comic horror and his cheeks puffed out as though they held a foul stew.

Back in the car, Louise said, "Well?"

"You want the truth?"

"Of course."

"He lusts for Ellie, but he's scared that lovemaking might injure the fetus. He knows it's irrational, but he can't help it. So he masturbates instead, thinking only of her. He thinks she's even more beautiful pregnant than she was before."

When we got home, Louise hurried upstairs to tell Ellie the good news. I probably should feel lousy for lying, but I know that Ellie doesn't really want the truth, even if she thinks she does. Most couples who have been married for a long time know intuitively that it's precisely their willingness to lie when it counts most that is the secret to their success. A hard fact for idealists to swallow, until they get married.

◆ ◆ ◆ ◆ ◆

You know the romance is dead when:

1) You floss your teeth together.

2) Serious emotions, even lust, are expressed in baby talk.

3) You know what she will say before she says it, and this does not delight you.

4) You do not tell her she looks beautiful even when she does.

6) Secrets are your most intimate companions.

7) What used to drive you crazy about her drives you crazy about her.

8) You refill her wine glass only because you want her to fall asleep early.

9) You sacrifice the truth for peace and quiet.

◆　◆　◆　◆　◆

After what I did to Starla, I was too ashamed to linger in bed with her, and so I hustled her to a booth in a local Chinese restaurant, where I attempted to assuage my guilt with sound advice. I told her that showing up at the apartment of a complete stranger and undressing within minutes was stupid and reckless. She had no business answering grown-up personal ads. She was just a kid.

"I don't like boys my age," she whispered. Her eyes went dreamy, and she flicked her tongue along the shaft of her egg roll. I realized for the first time that she might be certifiably insane, capable of anything, including having me thrown in jail for twenty-five years. I paid the check and practically frog-walked her to the nearest subway stop. She refused to walk through the turnstile until I had kissed her on the mouth.

As we separated, she breathed, "I want you so bad."

The next afternoon, the phone awakened me out of a shallow nap. Starla said that she had told her mother and grandma all about our date and they thought I was a "fine man" for sending her home. She joked that if I was so worried about her age, maybe I should date her mother instead. She was only twenty-eight. I was struck dumb with shame. Before we hung up, she made me promise to call her if I ever got lonely.

In fact, I had never felt so lonely in all my life. A lot of guys might have made the mistake of kissing Starla, but how many, after learning her real age, would have done what I did? Very few, I thought, and no one I would care to know. Who was I then? Who, really? My heart was in the right place. I gave money to charity. I stood with the oppressed wherever and whenever they huddled. But none of this mattered now that I knew the truth about myself. I wasn't one of the good guys.

I never had been. If I had lived before the Civil War, I would certainly have owned slaves and raped them.

I began to disintegrate. During the day I still polished the already shining toilets of my ugly millionaire, but at night I holed up in my apartment, drinking Scotch and smoking myself green in front of the TV. I brooded over my losses, not just of Ilene but of all the others—my favorite grandmother to bone cancer, my father to suicide, and my mother to a series of boyfriends each more useless than the last. I relived the heartbreaks of high school, and sometimes, even, the playground. My self-pity was bottomless. I was convinced I would never know another moment's happiness and, worse, that I did not deserve to.

Finally, I sought out a psychiatrist. I often wonder how much I might have grown had I committed to the therapeutic process right then and there. Instead I was sidetracked after just a few sessions by a telephone call from a college pal who was coming to Manhattan and needed a sublet through mid-August. Although my rent was seven hundred dollars a month, I told him that he could have my place for twelve hundred. I was stunned when he immediately agreed.

The next thing I knew I had bought a plane ticket for Rome. I lacked the clarity to understand that I was fleeing my life. In fact, I told myself that I was bravely confronting it, venturing off in search of images of beauty with which to kindle my imagination. Enough of women. Enough of love. It was only in the crucible of absolute loneliness and under the influence of great art that my young talent would be forged into genius.

◆ ◆ ◆ ◆ ◆

I gave Louise her usual Valentine's Day gift of tulips and truffles. She bought me *The Great Gatsby*. She thinks it is the first edition of 1925, worth a fortune, but it is merely the Modern Library edition from 1934, worth very little. Shopkeepers surely rub their hands together and drool when they see her coming.

♦ ♦ ♦ ♦ ♦

William Bolitho: "All adventure begins by running away from home."

♦ ♦ ♦ ♦ ♦

Ran into Mark Shankman, an old friend from Groton, as I cut through Central Park. I sat next to him on the bench and offered him a cigarette. Like me, he is a secret smoker, so he snatched it with equal parts hunger and shame. Remarkably sweet guy. I asked him what he was doing alone on a Wednesday afternoon. He said that he is the owner of a third-generation family business—a rigging company that engineers and executes the hoisting and placement of huge equipment atop buildings. He has all the money in the world, and all the time, too, as the business largely runs itself, but he is lonely. His wife died last year at forty-six and his twin sons attend college in California.

On days like today, he takes it easy and reflects, tries to figure out what he wants to do next. I told him it was pretty much the same for me. They used to call it a midlife crisis, I said, but that's a misnomer because we know we'll never live to a hundred. We're simply experienced enough now to know that time flies faster and faster as you age, and we want to chart a more meaningful course. He wholeheartedly agreed.

"Is it because we both married so young," I asked, "that we're in the exact same place?"

"No," he said, "my brother Dave never married, and he feels the same way. Except instead of taking afternoons off, he signs up for New Age workshops. Meditation. Kabbalah. Bullshit like that. He's lost."

Our talk was easy, not rushed. God bless whatever is slow. I can think of no better prayer for a New Yorker.

◆   ◆   ◆   ◆   ◆

My next wife, if there is one, must be a dedicated artist, so that we can serve as the guardians of each other's solitude. I would also want her to be intensely sensual because I intend to make up for lost time. Yet I do not want her to be insatiable, because that can be even more depressing than frigidity. I am not sure where I would ever meet such a woman. Not here in the library. Even if she walked in the door right now, I would never know. I almost never speak to strangers.

◆   ◆   ◆   ◆   ◆

Forgot to record an unsettling moment in my conversation with Mark Shankman. I told him that something he said senior year had had a big effect on me. One rainy Sunday, we were working at *The Circle Voice*, and he said, out of the blue, "Mal, why do you want to be a journalist? You're no journalist. You're a poet." I told him that until this moment it had never occurred to me that I could be a creative writer and that his comment really got me thinking. That summer I wrote my first short stories. When I started Yale in the fall, I declared

English as my major. I thought Mark might be touched to know that he had casually changed my life. He chuckled and said, "God, I sure hope I wasn't being sarcastic."

◆ ◆ ◆ ◆ ◆

Rereading this notebook, I recognize that I was unable to tell the story of Starla without first writing about Ilene. It must be because on some unconscious level I feel that the two are linked: Had Ilene not debased me I would never have debased Starla. Which is just another way of saying that had I trusted my intuition and dumped Ilene early on, she alone would have been hurt, but as I lacked the mettle, Starla and I suffered instead. Similarly, I feel now that I cannot tell the story of my courtship with Louise without first discussing the delicious Eva. The two are also linked somehow. I cannot prove it, but my imagination feels it to be true, and that's good enough for me.

◆ ◆ ◆ ◆ ◆

Today on my way to Melody Sandwich, a passerby stopped dead in mid-stride and looked at me. She was pretty in a Celtic way: fine cheekbones, green eyes, impish smile. Her upturned nose was red from the cold.

"You don't recognize me, do you, Mr. Poe? I temped for you four years and three months ago when your assistant Carol MacCready got married."

It took about five seconds of my staring at her like an imbecile before her name flew from my lips.

"Nora Woodley."

"Woodling. Good memory!"

"Yours is far better. You recognized me right off and got my name right."

"Come on, it was easy. How many editors badmouth their own magazines and offer their temps a shot of Scotch at quitting time?"

"More than you think."

She barked a laugh. "We had a blast, didn't we? Oodles of fun? Remember?"

"You're from rural Minnesota, aren't you?"

"Yup."

"Not bad, huh? For an old man of fifty."

"Fifty? Wow, you sure don't look it."

"Thanks."

"I'm about to turn forty."

"You don't look it either."

"That's because I'm thirty-eight. I always add a year. Oh, by the way—" She gave me a playful punch on the arm. "That's for firing me."

"I didn't fire you."

"Fibber."

"Carol got back from her honeymoon."

"Nope, she still had two weeks left."

"Are you sure?"

"Positive. Oops, I'm gonna be late for work."

"I'll walk you."

We headed north at a brisk pace, our breaths visible in the cold air. I let her take a slight lead so that I could get a better look at her. Her body is small and slenderly wonderful. She swings her arms when she walks. A marvelous head of short ginger hair.

"Where do you work?" I asked.

"An antiques store called the Salem House. Just a few

blocks that-a-way. What about you? Still at *Investors Monthly*?"
She pulled out a lace hanky and pinched it to her nose.

"Nope, I quit a few weeks ago."

"To write your novel?"

"Why do you say that?"

"That was your dream."

"Wow, your memory really is splendid."

"You made a big impression on me. I worshiped the ground
you walked on. I did! You were so literate and confident. I'm
hopeless with grammar and my spelling is positively woeful."

"Sometimes a sign of genius."

As we crossed the avenue, I laid my hand on the small of her
back and confessed that I had not quit, but had actually been
forced to take early retirement. She grinned and quoted *Julius
Caesar* about how some have greatness thrust upon them.

"Greatness?"

"Sure, it's much better to be fired than to quit. You got
severance, right?"

"Right."

"Which means you're getting paid to write. What's better
than that?"

The Salem House is a tasteful little place. In the front
window, a man wearing a dark pin-striped suit and a pink
tie fussed with a display of antique jewelry. When he saw
Nora, he pursed his lips and tapped the crystal of his shiny
gold watch. Nora quickly thanked me. I promised to pop in
sometime.

Heading back to Melody Sandwich, there was a bounce
in my step and openness in my heart that I have not felt in
years. Hardly surprising that Nora has awakened so much joy
in me. The reason I fired her was not that she lacked office
skills, although she did. It's that I was falling in love with her,

and the secret of my monogamy has always been to avoid temptation at all costs.

◆   ◆   ◆   ◆   ◆

As I got into bed a few hours ago, Louise laughed at my night guard. She said I looked like a teenage girl with a retainer. I felt like backhanding her into the lamp. A completely insane response. It shook me so deeply that I could not sleep. My mind went straight to Nora. You would think that so many years apart would have ended my crush or at the very least had no effect on it at all, but it seems actually to have intensified it. I am like one of those drunks who quit drinking for years, but then go back on the bottle only to discover that their disease has dangerously progressed. I smiled, remembering how Nora had tried to cheer me with "Some are born great, some achieve greatness, and some have greatness thrust upon them," but then I realized with a jolt that the line is not from *Julius Caesar*. I grew agitated. What play was it? The fact that I did not know felt symptomatic of everything wrong with my life. I jumped out of bed and hurried down here. Chuck trotted at my heels. Refusing to rely on Google, I made straight for my Yale Shakespeare. Four Scotches, six cigarettes, and two hours later, I am whole again. It is from *Twelfth Night*.

◆   ◆   ◆   ◆   ◆

Despite the impending blizzard, Louise and Karen are spending Saturday in the city—art museum, lunch, and a musical. I pretended to brood that I had been left out, but I was jubilant. The house all to myself. I am surely the happiest unemployed person in America. My imagination and talent are all the treasure I need. I doubt if I would feel this way if Louise were not so wealthy, and if, right after we got married, she had not insisted that I keep my entire salary for myself in a separate bank account to use for incidentals.

The whole world worries about money, but I and my family are immune. What a gift. Thank heaven the bulk of the Carver fortune is in treasuries. Although I will soon be excluded from it, I do have my savings, my exit bonus, my pension, Social Security, and perhaps a sizable divorce settlement. I am proud and pleased that during these hard economic times, I will be living the spartan life of an artist and not sitting in our empty nest with my pampered wife and our loyal help, with no greater worry than whether to paint the trim of our estate seashell, sheep's wool, or parchment white.

♦ ♦ ♦ ♦ ♦

On that fateful morning, I lugged my backpack into the train station at Nice. My rail pass allowed me unlimited train travel, but because it was summer, the overnight trains were almost always packed, which meant that whenever I traveled at night—something which, for economy's sake, I tried to do as often as possible—I was forced to sleep either on the grimy floor between the seats or on the even grimier floor outside the compartment. A few times I even settled for the steel luggage rack above the seats, which did nothing for my optimism or feelings of self-worth.

Given my condition that morning, it's a wonder Louise did not throw up at the sight of me. In the past forty days, I had not eaten a meal inside or slept in a bed; I had bathed almost solely in the Mediterranean, and I had not laundered my clothes. My only luxury was my journal into which I dumped the whole crazy riot of my imagination. If Louise's goal had been to tempt me into falling in love with her, she could not have appeared at a more propitious moment. I spotted her almost at once, prattling with three girlfriends. Her friends wore cut-offs and college T-shirts. Louise wore a dress—blinding white against her sunburned skin and lemon-bleached hair.

We had met seven months before, back in Manhattan, when she and a few of her friends from Sarah Lawrence had crashed a pal's Christmas party. Of the group, she was the one I'd found the least interesting. We met again a few days later when the same pal dragged me along on a double date to the Plaza. While the other couple laughed and flirted, anticipating a clash of genitals, Louise and I rolled candle wax between our fingers and hardly spoke. A funny-faced marketing major from a rich Republican family was the farthest thing from my type, and evidently an unpublished writer who trudged through life beneath a yoke of poverty and self-loathing was the antithesis of hers. It was only through the grapevine, days later, that I learned the actual reason for Louise's shyness: She thought I was the most beautiful, brilliant man she had ever met. My charisma had ripped out her tongue. More queasy than flattered, I made a mental note to avoid her at all costs.

In Nice, however, there was only the here and now, in which Louise Jane Carver, spunky, clean, well fed, and rich, embodied everything that I lacked. What choice did I have but to let her buy me a hot meal?

"Hey, pretty girl," I said.

"Oh...my...God!" she cried. "Malcolm! You have a beard! What are you doing in France?"

"Traveling."

She reacted with slack-jawed amazement as though I had not just stated the obvious.

"Me too!"

Her inability to detect sarcasm would serve me well.

"I just got back from Aix-en-Provence!" she screamed. "I studied Impressionism!"

"*Incroyable.* That means incredible." She threw her arms around my neck. Nothing attracts a frantic woman more surely than a man who offers little, and so I smoked a cigarette in almost total silence while she told me in spastic bursts all about her summer courses and how they had sparked in her a new ambition. No longer could she be content working in public relations. It was trivial and soulless. Now she wanted to work in public relations *for an art museum.*

"Much better," I said. "It's creative."

Batting her albino lashes, she asked what I was up to. I told her that I had no itinerary. I was just bumming around on six bucks a day, sleeping on trains and in city parks, absorbing local sights and sounds, while my novel took shape in my imagination. She asked what the book was about, and I muttered through a filthy cloud, "Everything and nothing." Her eyes flashed and she invited me to stay with her in Paris. In her hotel room. I sucked a deep drag and exhaled slowly as though I were mulling it over.

"You headed there now?" I asked.

She rolled her eyes. "I wish. I have to go shoe shopping in Milan with my crazy Aunt Bunny. I don't get to Paris till Friday night. Can you meet me?"

I took out my journal and a pen. "Which hotel?"

"I don't know yet. My mom's booking it. Pick a place where you and I can meet."

"Notre Dame. Saturday at noon."

"It's a date." She pecked me on the lips. Her breath smelled of Orangina. She ran toward the gates, knees knocking and wings flapping like a tall bird taking off on ice.

"Saturday at noon!" I shouted.

"I'll be there, mister!"

I spent the week in Nice, reading *The House of Mirth*, for which I had traded, on a nude beach in Greece, *Women in Love*, for which I had traded, on a streetcar in Naples, *In Our Time*. When I wasn't reading, I wandered the streets, gnawing on cheap salami and bread and scribbling in my notebook. At night I slept on the stony beach, while all around me kids danced, took drugs, made music, got drunk, shed clothes, and swallowed fire. It was an indigent circus for the affluent tourists who lined the sea wall, gawking and cheering and lusting. At midnight, after they had they returned to their grand hotels, we crawled into our dirty sleeping bags. Before dawn, the cops jabbed us awake with nightsticks so that the rich would emerge onto their balconies to a postcard view.

Such is the power of deprivation that by the time I had reached Paris, I had convinced myself that Louise was a rare and vibrant spirit—an ideal partner for a brooding man of letters. I even longed for her sexually. Falling asleep on the lumpy beach at Nice, I imagined myself kissing her queer, lipless face, wrapping myself in those lanky limbs, driving her to the heights of orgasm. But just as rapturous to me as any images of our sex were dreams of what came with it: starched sheets, cold champagne, a flush toilet, domed delicacies wheeled in by snooty French bellmen.

Saturday was gray and humid. I spent the morning in a public bathroom, washing my armpits, shampooing my hair, and trimming my beard. I arrived at Notre Dame ten minutes early, wearing filth-crusted jeans and my last clean T-shirt—

ironically, a promotional gift that had arrived the day before I left, from *Chocolate Kisses*. At noon, there was no sign of Louise. When one o'clock passed, I was sick with fear. By two o'clock, I was on the verge of neural collapse. Aside from my bewilderment and hurt, I couldn't bear the thought of one more minute spent in my own stinking flesh. I slouched into the cathedral to mourn my loss in the cool of its consecrated shadows.

A choir sang.

I fell into a pew, head bowed, waiting for holy music to purge me of my wretchedness. After a few seconds, I realized with a start that the chant was in English. I checked a paper program on the floor. A boys chorus from Philadelphia. I had come halfway around the world for this? Clearly, the universe was mocking me. I closed my eyes again, desperate for oblivion. That's when I heard a tiny, moist sound—strange but distinctly human. I looked over, and standing in the aisle just a few feet away was a beautiful dark girl. She was staring at me, trying to speak, but fear had drained her mouth. The sound I had heard was the pasty smacking of thick saliva against dry lips. Finally, she got up the nerve and asked if the spot next to me was taken. I shook my head.

As she sat down, I thought, My God, look what Louise's absence has delivered to me.

"I'm Malcolm," I whispered.

"I am Eva."

♦ ♦ ♦ ♦ ♦

Today at the gym, an art dealer named Mike Rapisarda, perhaps forty-five, sharp and funny, told me between bench presses that his new year's resolution was to stop sleeping with girls under thirty. He claimed that as hot as these young babes are, he must break the habit, because they don't know the rules. I asked which rules. He said the unspoken ones that govern grown-up sex. For instance, during foreplay there is often an awkward moment as you unbuckle your belt or kick off your shoes. A grown woman takes this in stride. A girl bursts out laughing and spoils the mood. If a woman experiences, say, the taste of garlic in her mouth, she will slip unnoticed into your bathroom and discreetly rummage for mouthwash. The young girl announces in mid-kiss "Oh God! My breath stinks! Can I borrow a toothbrush?" When the sex is over, the grown woman knows that she must offer to go home, whereupon the man will either help her to gather her things or insist that she spend the night. The young girl curls up on your chest and starts planning where you'll eat breakfast. Mike claims that these faux pas leave him feeling lonely and disgusted when he ought to be doing postcoital cartwheels.

◆　◆　◆　◆　◆

Sick and tired of spending my lunch hours outside Melody Sandwich, I dropped by the Salem House instead. The owner, William C. Rhodes, informed me that Wednesday is Nora's day off.

"Shoot," I said, "I was hoping to take her to lunch."

He gave me the old fish eye and said, "She doesn't eat out. She brings a sandwich."

"Really? Because just the other day, I ran into her at lunch hour on Forty-Third and—"

"Doctor's appointment."

"Oh."

He glanced without subtlety at my wedding ring. To prove that I was no threat, as well as to punish him for his presumption, I spent a full half hour browsing the estate jewelry, asking dozens of stupid questions. His face got so red with impatience that I thought he would burst a blood vessel. It was not a complete charade, however, as my wedding anniversary looms, and it's a biggie. I told him that I was in a pickle because Louise does not wear silver jewelry, but he insisted that the rules for which gifts to give on which anniversaries are antiquated rubbish. It behooved him to say this, of course, because he sells mostly gold and platinum. I pretended that I was just about to buy a twelve-thousand-dollar diamond brooch, but then at the last minute I backed out. The look on his puss was priceless. If Nora works on commission, I'll buy Louise's gift from her. If not, I will shop elsewhere. I believe William C. Rhodes is the first gay man I have ever met with no sense of humor. Like finding a lesbian with one.

♦ ♦ ♦ ♦ ♦

Open-jacket weather. The sky an intricate, mottled cotton.

♦ ♦ ♦ ♦ ♦

This morning I discovered a lump on the left side of my neck. Because it is on the same side as the ear infection I had last Christmas, I am fairly sure that it's just a swollen lymph node and there's no need to worry. Still, lump is a lump is a lump. I also felt a deep ache in my kidney today, but I assume the two are unrelated.

♦ ♦ ♦ ♦ ♦

A contemporary *Robinson Crusoe*, only there is no Friday and the island is Manhattan.

◆ ◆ ◆ ◆ ◆

Socrates: "By all means, marry. If you get a good wife, you'll be happy; if you get a bad one, you'll become a philosopher."

◆ ◆ ◆ ◆ ◆

Rebuttal to Annie: Examples of great artists who put their families before their work are rife, but no one knows about these heroes, because their names sink into the sands of obscurity, leaving not a trace behind, not a footprint, except the glow of well-being on the faces of their happy children.

◆ ◆ ◆ ◆ ◆

Overheard on the subway: "Stalin smoked four packs a day and stank of tobacco. He stank of alcohol, too. Being a Georgian he didn't drink vodka. Just wine. Hitler had a stomach problem that gave him gas, and his vegetarianism only made it worse. Now Mao was really smelly. Did not bathe or brush his teeth. Rarely wiped his big butt. You could smell him from clear across the room. He used to say 'Why should I wash my dick? I wash it in a new girl every night!'"

◆ ◆ ◆ ◆ ◆

How to explain the sudden alchemy: This book, once a mere narcissistic indulgence, has been transmuted into an artist's journal—a sketch pad of studies, plots, insights, notions, asides, epigraphs, jokes, and fancies. It will be an invaluable resource to me as I begin my first major work.

♦ ♦ ♦ ♦ ♦

I could not believe my eyes. There she was walking toward me: Starla Ferris. I threw down my cigarette and raced to her, perhaps a bit too excitedly, because when she saw me coming, she lifted an arm as though to fend off an attacker.

"Don't be afraid!" I laughed. "It's me, Starla! Malcolm! From *Chocolate Kisses!*"

When her face went blank, I realized that, although this was certainly the same woman I had seen in line, it was not Starla Ferris.

I stepped away at once. "I'm so sorry. I thought you were somebody else."

"That's all right," she said.

Her speech was polished, not even remotely street. She tried to walk on, but I blocked her way.

"You look so much like my friend. It's uncanny. You don't happen to know a Starla Ferris, do you?"

The minute the question left my lips, I regretted it.

As though all blacks know one another! She dismissed me with a polite smile and walked inside. The swarthy owner of the sandwich shop, standing there with a customer, had overheard the entire thing. When we locked eyes, he frowned and made a shooing gesture with his cigarette as though I were a homeless pest. I could not have felt more disgraced.

While I'm heartsick that I may never have a chance to apologize to Starla for what I did, I console myself with the fact that she was a child when we met and that she has probably forgotten the whole episode—either because time heals all wounds or because the wounds that followed were so much deeper and ghastlier. It also occurs to me that I might have her name wrong. Maybe it's Stella. Maybe it's Farris. Or Garris. It's possible. It's been so long. When I think of the hours I wasted outside the sandwich shop, I'm furious with myself. How could I be so profligate with time when the future is so pressing?

◆   ◆   ◆   ◆   ◆

I know that I ought to be in psychotherapy right now, but I keep putting it off—not because I am resistant to growth, but because I fear the cost. I don't mind spending the lion's share of my savings on a co-op apartment, for example, but my Protestant nature bridles at an extra $200 a week for a shrink who might turn out to be crazier than I am.

This morning I found myself walking down the central corridor of a public mental-health clinic, in search of a therapist at a bargain-basement price. Outside the employment office, I spotted a messy bulletin board where a notice caught my eye: "Do you like to talk on the phone and are you good with people?" The answer to both, for me, was a resounding no, especially lately, but I kept reading. The notice said that the local branch of the State Suicide Help Line is looking for someone to answer calls part-time. It's hard to imagine a better job for a novelist. What, after all, is a novel but a sustained argument against suicide?

The minimum requirement for the job is a college degree in either psychology or sociology. I ducked inside and filled out an application, telling the truth as often as I could. I invented a master's degree in social work. As there's not a chance in hell that a clinic from which I am receiving discount therapy would consider hiring me to help others, I ended my search for help. I will find a shrink elsewhere.

◆ ◆ ◆ ◆ ◆

Tonight Louise begged me to be her date for the final lecture at the Morrow Estate. Ellie had her baby last night (it's a Gardner!), so without me Louise would be forced to go solo. I told her that as much as I would love to be of use, I was in no mood to pick over the bones of the dead, even ones as comely as those of the late, great Helen Hayes.

"Fine," she said, "but if some dark, handsome stranger whisks me off my feet, don't say I didn't give you a chance to prevent it."

"I won't," I said, with a dead seriousness that would have sent shivers through any sentient being.

As soon as she drove off, I bounced into Karen's bedroom doorway. "Hey, sweet thing, let's get pizza."

She yanked out an ear bud. "What did you say?"

"Let's get pizza."

Karen and I share a love of pizza. She loves it because it is delicious and vegetarian, I love it merely because it's delicious. Louise and the other girls reject it because it is fattening. Karen doesn't care that it is fattening because plumpness is a badge of honor to young feminists.

As we gobbled down a family-size half-vegetable/half-sausage, we struggled to make conversation. It abruptly dawned me that we have grown so far apart that perhaps pizza is all we have in common. It happens suddenly. One minute you're the hip, fun parent to whom they can talk about anything, and the next you're the embarrassing doofus who's never heard of a single band on her playlist. When Karen mentions a singer she loves, and I draw a blank, she makes the same face I made when my senile grandmother first called me by the name of her kid brother who died at the Battle of the Bulge.

The most unsettling aspect of the whole thing is that middle age is not a prison from which there is no escape. All I'd have to do is watch a few mindless TV shows, read a few shitty books and magazines, browse a few time-guzzling websites, and I could be fun and hip again, but a prime symptom of middle age is that you lose patience. You simply cannot be bothered to waste a single minute of your precious time reading *Celebrity Scum* magazine or downloading the musical antics of a band of plagiaristic clowns.

Although Karen is by no means pretty (her mustache is growing in nicely, thank you), I'm far more at ease with her in public than I was with her sisters at her age. Sarah and Annie were so gorgeous as teenagers that every guy who laid eyes on them posed a potential threat. When we walked through Times Square, I was like a middle linebacker, crouched over, eyes bugging, head on a swivel. Karen does not attract predators. The sort of man who would go for Karen is in a laboratory right now, blinking into a physics book, or in his basement, clacking away at a keyboard while he tugs at himself. He is years away from the sort of social confidence required to maintain an erection inside the warm body of an actual female. Anyway, I have not the slightest doubt that Karen will find a wonderful girlfriend at college. In their first year of licking each other, ten pounds will fall off their hips like sacks of granola, and they will live happily ever after.

Something is wrong with me. What kind of man writes what I just wrote? Maybe this is more freedom than I can bear. Has my brain become a devil's playground?

◆ ◆ ◆ ◆ ◆

Dinner at the Whites. Aidan and Tina Fitzroy were there.
At one point, I looked around the table and, interrupting
someone's small talk, grumbled, "Six. Perfect. Just enough for
Russian Roulette." Dead silence. All the way home, Louise
struggled to forgive me. My silence did not make it easy.
Later, sitting at her vanity table, wiping off her make-up, she
asked why I could not have at least pretended to be interested
in what anyone else had to say. She looked so sad that I felt a
pang of guilt. I led her by the hand to the bed and made love to
her. Her orgasm was so violent that Chuck barked. I was afraid
he would awaken Karen from her dreams of practical shoes.
Afterward, Louise's mood was buoyant, almost exuberant. It
was only after I had escaped down here that I exhaled at last.
I would like to propose a toast, dear Chuck. To solitude, the
only cure for loneliness!

◆ ◆ ◆ ◆ ◆

When I dropped into the Salem House today, Rhodes was
busy with a customer, which gave me a chance to whisper to
Nora, "Do you work on commission?" She nodded yes. Then,
in a loud voice, I informed her that normally on anniversaries
I take the little lady out to dinner and a show, but as this was
the big 2-5, would she mind showing me some estate jewelry,
please? Nora said that she would be happy to.

   A cruel farce ensued, as for a full half-hour, knowing
full well that Rhodes was listening, I asked Nora to show me
the very same pieces that I'd had Rhodes show me last time
I was in the shop. Of course I asked the very same questions,
and when she answered roughly as he had, I pretended that I

had never heard the answers before. By the end, Rhodes's face looked like a blood blister.

Nora commented that I seemed awfully cavalier. It was such an important occasion, and yet I seemed willing to buy just about anything she showed me. I explained that Louise is a product of tremendous wealth. As a child she never lacked for anything but love and attention. For her twelfth birthday she received a pony, for her thirteenth a horse. As a result, there was nothing material under the sun that excited her that she had not already bought or been given. So whether I picked the ruby-encrusted brooch or the 18-karat charm bracelet mattered not a jot. All that mattered was the thought behind it. And the card, of course. Louise loved cards.

Finally, I chose the charm bracelet, because it was a thousand dollars cheaper than the brooch. Before I signed the sales slip, I looked over at Rhodes and saw the same sort of apprehension in his eyes that I had seen in those of Doug Viertel before I signed my exit papers. Rhodes needed to pay his rent and was afraid I might change my mind again.

"I'll sign on one condition," I said, loud enough for him to hear. "You have to have lunch with me, Miss Woodling. Right now."

Shocked, she stammered: "But it's only eleven-fifteen."

I looked at Rhodes. "What do you say, Willy? You want the sale or not?"

Rhodes forced a smile and said fine, run along.

Nora walked with me in complete silence for two full blocks before she confessed that she felt uncomfortable having lunch with a married man, especially one just weeks away from his twenty-fifth wedding anniversary. That was my cue to insist that my intentions were honorable, but I couldn't do it. I'm tired of lying.

My explanation took up our entire meal. Nora did not utter a word, just listened, wearing a serious look that leant even more soulfulness to her already lovely face. If Louise had found herself in a similar situation, she would have repeatedly interjected, finding some way to bring the subject back to herself, even if just by offering saintly support. Nora felt no such urge. I told her the whole truth about my doomed marriage, even many of the details of which I am most ashamed.

For example, I told her that almost a decade ago I had decided that I would escape my marriage the day after my youngest started college. As a result, last fall when it was time for Karen to apply, I had subtly guided her toward schools that began their fall terms in mid-August rather than early September. In other words, I was willing to compromise my daughter's education in order to pick up an extra week or two of freedom for myself. If Nora found this as petty and contemptible as I did, she did not let on.

When I was finished, Nora sat in silence for a few long seconds before asking me why I had married Louise in the first place.

"That's for another time," I said.

On the way back to the shop, she shrank into silence again.

"Do you think I'm despicable?" I asked.

Tears rose to her eyes. "No, I think you're a fine person. Most men who believe in divorce would have left a long time ago, but you stayed for the sake of your children. Self-sacrifice is so rare these days. We live in selfish times, Mr. Poe."

"Malcolm."

She smiled wistfully. "Not as long as you're married."

"Fair enough. Say you'll have lunch with me again."

"You're really going to move out as soon as Karen starts college?"

"Absolutely."

"And it's got nothing to do with me?"

"Nothing. I decided years ago."

"Then we can have lunch. But I want you to know that I'll be praying for you to save your marriage."

"You're religious?"

"Is that a problem?"

"Not at all. Maybe some of it will rub off on me."

Before we parted, Nora said that she was willing to have lunch with me just once a week. On Fridays. Walking back to the library, I realized that she needs to set an artificial limit on our time together only because she wants to see me so much more often. I believe she's falling in love with me.

♦ ♦ ♦ ♦ ♦

This morning as I was half-way way out the door, Louise came trotting down the stairs, all dolled up, announcing that she had an errand to run in the city. She told me not to ask her what the errand was, and then she threw me a big, fat comical wink that told me she was buying my anniversary gift today. I pretended to be charmed, but I was annoyed, because I knew what was coming next.

"Hold on, baby!" she said. "We'll take the train together."

I played fetch with Chuck for twelve endless minutes while Carmen fed Louise organic oatmeal, fruit salad, Greek yogurt, and herbal tea.

The ride into the city was the usual torture of my trying to read the *Times* while Louise chitchatted on a wide array of tiresome subjects.

Then, suddenly, I was snapped alert by this: "Mal, isn't that Tom from work?"

I looked over and sure enough Tom Feldsher was sitting across the aisle, six rows down. Louise started to wave to him, but I yanked her arm down so hard that I almost dislocated it.

"Ow!"

"I don't want him to see us."

"Why not?"

"He's an asshole."

"Since when?"

"Since he started cheating on Cindy."

"No!"

"Be quiet."

"But I talked to Cindy at the Christmas party. They were loving the empty nest. They were planning a second honeymoon. How do you know he's cheating?"

"I caught them in a conference room."

"It's someone at the office? Why didn't you tell me?"

"A male thing. You never snitch. Anyway, maybe the affair'll blow over."

"Who's the girl?"

I could have chosen anyone, but I went with the first slut who popped into my mind.

"Juliet Hacker."

"The pretty one with the great laugh?"

"Great, if you like migratory birds."

Tom finally saw us and waved. Louise, reflexively forgiving, grinned and waved back. So did I, but as my shoulder rose, I felt a stabbing pain. The lump in my neck was acting up. And no wonder. I knew if we exchanged even a few words with Tom, he was certain to bring up my firing. We have not spoken since I cleared my desk.

The moment the train pulled into the station, before Tom had even had a chance to stand up, I grabbed Louise by the wrist and dragged her out the back doors. Rather than arouse her suspicion, my erratic behavior actually impressed her. She said not many men would end a friendship over a buddy's infidelity. Most would just pump him for dirty details. I was so relieved to have averted disaster that I was fairly giddy by the time I found her a taxi. I gave her a fast hug and kiss, but then, just as she was getting in the car, she mentioned she was lunching today with Iris Viertel. I felt like crying as the cab roared away. I love my furlough. I don't want it to end.

I was too anxious to read or write, so instead I wandered the cold streets. At the Salem House, I waved to Nora through the foggy window. She smiled back, but I quickly walked away. It is only Wednesday. I don't want her to think me overeager. I eventually ducked into a movie theater, but it was hard to enjoy the film due to my worry and my throbbing lump. My phone vibrated the moment I emerged from the darkness. It was Louise calling, but I did not have the courage to pick up.

In a few minutes, my train will be pulling into the station. Rather than take a cab over the bridge, I will take the bus—a little extra time to get my story straight. Given that Doug lied to me about keeping my voicemail active, it is inconceivable to me that he did not tell Iris everything. And of course Iris discussed it with Louise. Most wives would be enraged to discover that their husband had deceived them over something as vital as employment, but not Louise. No, she will be merely wounded, unable to fathom that I could be so selfish as to deprive her of the opportunity to comfort me. She will not say it, of course. She will say, "Mal, why? Why didn't you tell me? Did you really think I wouldn't understand?" Then she will tell me that I am still a young man and that it's time for me to roll up my sleeves, pull myself up by my boot-straps, and get back on the bike. Or the horse. No one wields clichés like Louise. Each one maims me. Shit, there she is. Waiting on the platform. In the snow. Dear God, what a mess.

♦ ♦ ♦ ♦ ♦

I spoke first: "You didn't have to pick me up."

"But, honey, it's freezing out."

"You're so sweet."

"So are you."

"No, I'm not. How was your day?"

"Not bad. Not bad at all."

"Lunch with Iris was fun?

"She's blue. Dolly ran away."

"Who's that?"

"Her bichon frisé."

"What's that?"

"A dog, silly."

"I thought it was a lettuce."

"And Cheri, their eldest, had an abortion."

"Good for her."

"The father's one of her professors at Vassar. He's thirty-nine and Chinese and married and shorter than she is. Some sort of expert on Ming ceramics. He offered to pay child support, but Iris and Doug put their foot down, and Cheri aborted. Afterward, she went horseback riding and bled so bad she needed a transfusion."

"And a brain transplant."

"We hit the jackpot with our girls. Knock wood."

Louise rapped the leather steering wheel.

I studied her face, looking for some sign that Iris had spilled the beans about my firing. She seemed a little more subdued than usual, but that was all. And yet my worry did not subside.

During dinner Karen asked, "Why are you staring at Mom like that?"

"She's my chattel. I can do whatever I want."

Louise laughed, but Karen did not.

"I didn't tell you to stop staring," Karen said. "I just asked why."

"Well, if you must know it's because your mom looks particularly fetching tonight, and I was wondering what her secret is."

Karen squinted, smelling a rat.

Louise laid a hand on mine. "Do I have the awesomest husband in the world or what?"

"Mom, please stop that."

"What?"

"Talking like a teenager. It's mortifying. Not even the biggest loser at school says 'awesomest.'"

♦ ♦ ♦ ♦ ♦

If I push on my lump with two fingers, I see stars. One hopeful fact is that cancer seldom hurts this badly. At least not in the early stages. I'll call Dr. Warder and leave a message on his service. Normally I would wait a few days, but my stool has been tapering again.

♦ ♦ ♦ ♦ ♦

"It's not the ocean that gets you, it's the puddles." I am not sure what this means, but it just came to me. A book of short stories called *Puddles*.

♦ ♦ ♦ ♦ ♦

Shakespeare: "What fool is not so wise to lose an oath to win a paradise?" Is the Bard endorsing divorce here? It is merely anecdotal, but it seems that adultery is all the rage right now. Off the top of my head, there is the heart surgeon who left his wife for a Cuban lawyer who happens to be male; the hedge fund manager whose wife left him for a smelly, penniless painter; the owner of the revival movie theater who left his wife for the Goth fatso who tears the tickets; the writer whose mentally ill wife abandoned him and their two daughters for the idiot son of a Republican congressman; and on and on and on. Each story is more sad and absurd than the last, and yet Louise derives some sort of demented satisfaction from them. It must be the same happiness that the healthy feel when a cripple wheels past or a shrouded gurney is slammed into the back of an ambulance or a friend's friend comes down with ALS. These tragedies are a reminder that our marriage abides. That her life has amounted to something. That she is winning.

♦ ♦ ♦ ♦ ♦

Introspection is the leading cause of insomnia. Louise sleeps like the dead.

♦ ♦ ♦ ♦ ♦

At the gym, while bench-pressing a full tenth of my body weight, I overheard the following: "I love life, just not the one I'm living." Not bad, I thought. I smiled at the speaker, a beautiful kid with a mop of brown curls and a bright, vivid face, wearing a tight black T-shirt that said "Trainer." He saw me staring and asked if I'd had my complimentary fitness evaluation yet.

"Nope."

"How long have you been a member?"

"Only eleven years. Listen, I know the drill. You give me the evaluation, then shame me into buying a package of training sessions at a hundred bucks an hour. No thanks."

"Eighty-five," he said, walking over and extending a hand. "Hi, I'm Archie."

If his first name had been the only thing he shared with my son, it wouldn't have even occurred to me, but now that he stood closer I saw my son's big brown eyes and absurdly long lashes and cupid's-bow mouth. It is not an exaggeration to say that had Archer lived, he might have looked very much like this young man.

"Come on, the evaluation's free," he said. "What have you got to lose?"

My peace of mind, I thought, as I fled to the showers. Some inner voice added: "What peace of mind?"

◆　◆　◆　◆　◆

The rest of Eva: In the cathedral of Notre Dame, I listened to the American choir for a little while, letting my nerves settle, then I unfolded my paper program and offered the girl a look at it. She leaned in close. Her breath was fragrant. Her skin was pale and smooth, her hair chestnut brown. Her eyes were a deep, dark blue. Some mouths you simply must kiss and hers was one of them. I dared a glance downward. Her turquoise tank top barely contained the swell of her ripe breasts. Her arms were lean and tanned. Her legs looked strong in their blue jeans. I wished I could find a flaw so that I could survive our inevitable parting.

"Where are you from?" she whispered.

"The United States," I answered. "You?"

"Norway."

"I would never have guessed."

"Not all of us are blond, you know."

"I guess not."

When the music ended, we stepped outside into a new day. The sky was blue now, the breeze cool, and the air tinged with gold. As we wandered, I asked her question after question. Eva's story, which as a result of her slow, precise English took her more than an hour to tell, went like this: For seven years, since she was thirteen years old, she had written to a pen pal, a rich Parisian boy two years her senior named René. They had a lot in common. Not only did they love the same books, bands, and films, but they also hated the same ones. As the years passed, their letters became more and more intimate, until it became a half-serious joke between them that one day they would marry. Their first meeting was planned for the summer Eva turned sixteen, but when the time came René's parents split up and his mother moved him to Montreal for college. Their correspondence had continued until just last week, when René moved back to Paris to live with his father. Days later, Eva boarded a train to meet him at long last.

It was like something out of a movie, she said. She descended the train with her rucksack and there he stood on the platform, better-looking than in any of his photographs. She melted into his arms and mouth as though it had happened a thousand times before. Equally familiar was her introduction into his home. René's father greeted her at the door as if she were his long-lost daughter. The first night was a perfect fantasy. A sumptuous meal for two, an empty apartment, candles everywhere. In a huge, gilded bedroom, Eva learned for the first time why it is sometimes called making love. The next morning when she awoke, René was not beside her. She emerged bleary-eyed into the living room and found him and his father, fully dressed, leaning over a map. On the floor was a row of matching designer suitcases.

"My father and I are going to Egypt," he announced.

"When?" she asked.

"Today."

No invitation, no explanation, no apology—and none demanded, for Eva was too shocked and humiliated to speak. Before they left for the airport, René handed her a key and said that she was welcome to stay there for as long as she liked. Shattered, she ate dry toast, repacked her bag, and left. On her way to the corner, she dropped the key down a sewer. She wasn't sure why. Rather than head home, she checked her bag at the train station and walked to Notre Dame, so that when she returned to Kongsberg she could tell her friends she had seen something other than René's bedroom ceiling.

Enter young Malcolm Willard Poe.

What struck me most powerfully was not Eva's story itself but rather the feelings it had inspired in me. Like most youths born to sick, selfish parents, I had never been much of a listener (why bother listening when all you're hearing is garbage?), but I hadn't been aware of the deficiency until I found myself listening to Eva's story and living every minute of it, as though it were happening to me. When she finished, we were one person, both of us fighting tears. For the first time in my life, I had experienced empathy. I took her hand and told her how sorry I was. Within minutes, we were walking together, holding hands, laughing at the cruelty of René, and since neither of us understood how he could have done what he did, there was no more to be said.

As we circled back toward the cathedral, Eva and I decided that we would travel together. We were poor, but we both had train passes, which meant we could follow our hearts wherever they led us. We decided to start with Florence. We christened our union with a loaf of bread, a tomato, and a hunk of cheese, which we passed back and forth, taking bites and washing them down with slugs of warm cola. I knew already that I had been dead wrong. I hadn't come to Europe to be alone. I had come to fall in love. Loneliness was not the medium in which a young artist feels most truly alive, but that in which he feels the most secure. A far different thing. I felt exposed now, insecure, perhaps even in danger. How could it have been otherwise? For the first time in my life, I was giving my heart away. And I owed it all to daffy Louise. Thank God she had stood me up.

That's when I spotted Louise: in a panic, a hand to her mouth, running toward the cathedral, looking everywhere for me.

♦ ♦ ♦ ♦ ♦

Few human beings long to be immortal, but we all want our stories to be made timeless. This is why every single human being feels that his life would make a great book or movie if only it could be told in the right way. Hence the glut of shallow, disposable memoirs. The last thing the world needs is another one. I will write a novel.

♦   ♦   ♦   ♦   ♦

At our Friday lunch today, Nora Woodling reminded me of another afternoon four years ago. It was quitting time, and as usual I offered her a shot of Scotch, and, as usual, she refused. I poured the shot, anyway, and drank it along with my own. She said that it must have loosened my tongue, because a few minutes later I gazed out the thirtieth-floor window and, as though to roaring surf and not a canyon wall of glass, I recited all of "Dover Beach" from memory. "Ah, love, let us be true to one another! for the world, which seems to lie before us like a land of dreams, so various, so beautiful, so new, hath really neither joy, nor love, nor light..." She said it was the most romantic thing that had ever happened to her, only she wasn't sure whether I was reciting it to her or to the cosmos. As flattered as she was, she hoped it was to the latter. I was, after all, a married man.

When I fired her a few days later, she knew that I couldn't have been reciting the poem to her. She was sad to leave my employ, but relieved that she had not witnessed a "near occasion of sin."

Hearing this, I decided to go for broke. I set down my knife and fork and threw back a fortifying gulp of beer.

"Prepare to be scandalized," I said. "The only reason I fired you was that I was falling in love with you, and it scared the hell out of me."

I got the feeling from her bug-eyed reaction that no man had ever told her that he loved her before. I was glad to be the first. With any luck at all, I would be the last. I reached across the table and took her damp, shy hand. It is terrible to admit, but I wondered in that instant if it had ever cupped a scrotum during intercourse.

"I was scared," I explained, "because Karen and Sarah were both still in high school at the time, and, as you know, I'd promised myself I wouldn't divorce Louise until all of my girls had graduated."

She silently removed her hand and went back to eating her salad, but her cheeks were pink now and her eyes filled with tumult. For the rest of the meal, we were like two timid teenagers, braving glances at one another.

Walking back to the shop, Nora and I discussed creativity. I explained that I have tremendous confidence and expect grand things from myself. If I do not have a novel published within a few years of leaving Louise, I will be absolutely gutted. She said that she expected big things from me, too. She asked what my novel will be about. Since I have no idea, I told her that I heed Goethe's advice: "Poet, don't talk." Nora smiled in a way that said, "Wow, a man who quotes Goethe."

Outside the Salem House, she scribbled something on a scrap of paper and handed it to me. She told me not to look at it until I got back to the library. As soon as I had turned the corner, I read it, hoping that it was romantic or erotic or both. It said "Jeremiah 29:11." I looked it up and was delighted: "'For I know the plans I have for you,' declared the LORD, 'plans to prosper you and not to harm you, plans to give you hope and a future.'"

◆ ◆ ◆ ◆ ◆

Annie turned twenty-four today. I sent her an email, filled with memories of what life was like when she was still in her mom's belly. I told her that in the beginning her mom was green with nausea every morning, noon, and night. The smell of everything, including me, sickened her. Whenever she marshaled the will to stand, she rang for Carmen. Soon the smell of garlic would waft through the house, and I'd find Louise alone in the den, wolfing down a pound of pasta— the only thing that brought her any relief. I joked that our baby was going to emerge wearing a macaroni bow tie and fettuccine scarf, smoking a ziti cigarette.

I concluded my letter by telling Annie that I loved her and that I hoped she and Joshua were happy and well. I have a hunch she knows just how hard this was for me to say. I am not sure whether to feel proud of myself for saying it or ashamed of my absolute lack of sincerity.

♦ ♦ ♦ ♦ ♦

Saw Dr. Warder today, fully expecting him to take one look at my lump and tell me that I was a paranoid lunatic. Instead, he said that while it was probably nothing serious, he was going to order an immediate MRI. Scared to death, I mentioned my tapering stool. He said they were unrelated and suggested an over-the-counter fiber pill. I offered to have an immediate colonoscopy. He laughed and said, "You just had one last year."

From what I have read, MRIs are highly unpleasant. Mine is scheduled for tomorrow morning, first thing. I won't tell Louise about it. Her optimism will only antagonize me.

♦ ♦ ♦ ♦ ♦

When did this book revert back to being a diary? God, I detest the quotidian. Especially mine.

♦　♦　♦　♦　♦

It is impossible, the night before a medical test that could deliver a death sentence, not to contemplate the worst. Let's say I am given just a few months to live, and I look back on my half century of life. What will have been its narrative? I was born, edited manuscripts, reared children, and died. Not enough. I must live while I have the chance!

♦　♦　♦　♦　♦

Before the MRI began, the pretty East Indian technician, I believe her name was Kiara, asked me three times if I was claustrophobic. The first time I said no. The second time it occurred to me that maybe I was and didn't know it. The last time, as she lowered a mask over my face, I cried, "Maybe! Maybe!" She asked if I would like headphones and music. For some reason, I declined. She braced my head so that I could not budge it. Suddenly I was moving down a conveyor belt. The chamber was narrower than a coffin. I couldn't move my arms. I also couldn't see a thing, except rainbow stickers and sparkly hearts—the sort of shit girls slap on their schoolbooks and bedroom doors in the months before their menarches. A terrible buzzing started, like something out of a horror film. I closed my eyes and tried desperately to clear my mind, enter a sort of Zen state, but all I could think about were the thousands of people who had lain precisely where I was lying, fairly certain that they were okay, only to emerge and learn that they had brain cancer. I began to hyperventilate. Clearly I was claustrophobic, but had not known it, for the simple reason that I had never been buried alive before. The machine was very loud. I couldn't breathe. I wanted out now. Now! I came unglued, whimpering like a baby. Dead at fifty. My girls without a daddy. No one to walk them down the aisle. Kiara crackled through the tiny speaker, "You're moving too much. I have to do the last one over."

♦   ♦   ♦   ♦   ♦

There is a website devoted entirely to the Native American names for the various monthly moons. Many would make remarkable titles for a novel: Snow Moon, Hunger Moon, Worm Moon, Blood Moon, Moon of Green Corn, Hunter's Moon, and Moon of Falling Leaves. Sadly, I doubt my novel will be rustic and unpretentious enough to warrant such a title. Like it or not, I am urban and sophisticated. A pale-face.

♦   ♦   ♦   ♦   ♦

I knew very early on, within days of Annie's birth, that no matter how happy or unhappy I was with Louise, I would never divorce her so long as there were children in the house. I had undergone far too much misery and neglect as the product of a broken home ever to impose similar anguish on my own kids. At the very minimum I would stay with Louise until the nest was empty, and I was fine with this. Fatherhood was wonderful. The only downside was the lack of time to write. After a long day at the office and two hours of daddy duty, I was lucky if I had the energy to brush my teeth, let alone hold a mirror up to America. It only got worse two years later when Sarah was born. Less than two years after that, Karen arrived. Archer came sixteen months later. With the birth of each child, the minimum lifespan of my marriage was extended and my writing ambitions became an ever more distant memory.

When Louise announced that four kids was enough and that she was going to tie her tubes, I made a mental note that the date of my earliest departure was set in stone now. Archer would start college when I was fifty-two. If I was happy in the marriage, I would naturally stay put; if I was not, I was free to go. I have never told anyone about this, but at Archer's funeral service, surrounded by sobbing family and friends, in some angry, inviolable corner of my brain, I made another mental note: the date of my earliest exit had abruptly changed. I could escape sooner now, when I was fifty.

◆　◆　◆　◆　◆

I just hung up with Dr. Warder. The lump is an infected lymph node, just as I'd first thought. Phew! He prescribed Amoxicillin and told me to expect diarrhea. I told him that I look forward to it, as the fiber pills weren't working. I ran upstairs to tell Louise my good news. Of course she took the whole thing with a grain of salt, laughing at my craziness. Even though I have begun the decade in which the luckiest die of heart attacks and the rest prepare for cancer, Louise never worries about my health. She insists that we will both live to be ninety. "We'll change each other's diapers," she jests. And I shudder.

I resolve to live in a more healthful way: eat better, smoke less, drink less, exercise more often. I don't ever want to be strapped into one of those machines again. I am convinced there are only two good ways to die: painlessly in your sleep, or hit by lightning while fucking.

◆　◆　◆　◆　◆

Princeton rejected Karen.

◆ ◆ ◆ ◆ ◆

Disastrous twenty-fifth-anniversary bash. Louise was impressed by the antique charm bracelet but crushed by my card. In my best penmanship, I had thanked her for being such a wonderful wife and mother and hailed her virtues with a parade of adjectives—loyal, kind, loving, devoted, selfless, etc. Even as I wrote them, I knew that she would far prefer sexy, irresistible, gorgeous, and exotic, but with one foot out the door, I've lost my taste for lying. As she read, her chin trembled and tears appeared in her eyes. Silly me, I thought she was touched, but then she croaked that it read like every single card I'd ever given her. I lost my temper, lashing out, telling her that she was out of her mind. Hands trembling, she retrieved a bunch of my old cards from her desk drawer and handed them over. Sure enough, they were almost word for word the same as the one I'd just given her.

She said a silver-anniversary card should be special, written from the heart with great care. Concealing my embarrassment, I told her I was unaware that Hoyle and the Marquess of Queensberry had ever weighed in on such matters. She had no idea what I was talking about, of course. Things got uglier from there. Soon Karen was locked in her room, (blaring Mucus Membrane or some other fabulous new rock band), Sarah was speeding in a taxi back to the train station, Louise was sniffling upstairs, Chuck was licking his balls, and I was sitting on the jungle gym, hitting the bottle pretty hard.

By the time Louise forced me inside to give me my gift, I was so drunk that I was barely able to muster a coherent word of thanks. It was a handmade leather album with a gorgeous photo from each year of our marriage. Most of the shots I had either forgotten or had never seen. There was one of Archer standing on my lap that was so heartbreaking I moved right past it. We went up to bed like old friends. She knew I was too drunk to make love so we just held each other for a while.

◆ ◆ ◆ ◆ ◆

The emptiness of this day in conjunction with the booze in my bloodstream has conspired to turn life into a slow, dumb dream.

◆ ◆ ◆ ◆ ◆

Maybe I will write a memoir disguised as a novel. There is so little difference. Once pen is set to paper, everything that follows is both the truth and a lie. Every serious writer knows this.

◆ ◆ ◆ ◆ ◆

Karen was rejected at both Stanford and Berkeley today. I dole her that I couldn't understand what she was crying about. Her guidance counselor had told her months ago that despite her verbal brilliance, her mathematical imbecility was going to make it tough for her to get into the very best schools. That's when Karen confessed that she hadn't believed it, that she had thought her extracurricular activities and essay would make a difference, and that's why she hadn't applied to any safety schools. I thought she was joking. When she showed me her list of colleges, I struggled to conceal my fury.

"It's no big deal," she said. "I'd rather take a year off than settle for mediocrity."

I asked her what she planned to do if she got in nowhere.

She shrugged her round dyke shoulders and said, "Live here, get a math skills, and reapply next year."

I have sacrificed everything for her, and yet there is now a possibility that she will exact another year of happiness from me.

◆ ◆ ◆ ◆ ◆

Rilke: "Surely all art is the result of having been once in danger." Boredom must be danger, because I long to create.

◆ ◆ ◆ ◆ ◆

In a period of ninety-six hours, Karen has been rejected by Harvard, Yale, Dartmouth, Penn, Swarthmore, Williams, Oberlin, Northwestern, Barnard, and Wesleyan. Everywhere but Brown! Lousy math scores or not, this made absolutely no sense to me, so I demanded that she show me her applications, something which she had stubbornly refused to do. She fought me tooth and nail all morning, but finally, in a torrent of tears, she threw them at me.

I soon discovered that her main essay, which she had used in one form or another at almost every school to which she applied, is on the subject of sarcasm, which she calls "the weapon of choice of the passive-aggressive." She makes her case with the portrait of a handsome, genial monster whose smiling barbs pluck flesh off everyone who dares cross his path. When confronted, he is clueless, a stranger to his own cruelty. What Karen has written is a portrait of me. No wonder she fought so hard to keep it from me.

Even putting my own wounded feelings aside, I can see that the essay is a dreadful piece of work. The prose is adequate and her insights are not without merit, but the tone is whiny and peevish. It is the work not of a gifted senior in need of higher education but of a twelve-year-old in need of an ass-thrashing. I can't imagine anyone reading this and wanting to meet her. In other words, barring divine intervention, Karen will be rejected by Brown as well. Louise will try to hide it, but she will be overjoyed to have her baby at home for another year. But me? What of me? How will I survive it?

◆ ◆ ◆ ◆ ◆

I am haunted by Karen's college essay and its dismal depiction of my fathering. I had no idea that I had hurt her feelings so often and so profoundly. If only she had spoken up. I mistook her masculinity for strength.

◆ ◆ ◆ ◆ ◆

Karen got into Brown! When she told me, I pranced around and shouted so loudly that she scrunched up her face and said, "Dad, chill out. *I* got in. Not you." I must hit their website right now and find out the dates of freshman orientation so that I can make my plans. I can't wait to tell Nora.

◆ ◆ ◆ ◆ ◆

My node is painless now, my stool fluffy and buoyant, and my prostate does not burn. I have not a single physical complaint. Could this be a harbinger of happiness?

◆ ◆ ◆ ◆ ◆

It is only April, but this book is full. Tomorrow is Easter. Rebirth, indeed!

BOOK TWO

Today was a celebration not only of Our Lord and Savior's return from the dead, but also of a far greater miracle: Karen's admission to an Ivy League school. Everyone attended our luncheon except for Annie, detained no doubt by the snapping, plunging pelvis of Joshua Mandel. (Why is it that whenever I imagine them making love, he is wearing his baseball cap, has a back scarred by acne, and finishes too quickly? Does this make me an anti-Semite?) As I jabbed my knife into the sizzling lamb roast, the phone chirped in the living room.

"Don't answer it," I commanded.

"It could be Poppo," Louise said as she rocketed from her chair.

"I know, that's why I said it."

She checked the caller ID and sure enough it was Bastard Bill, calling from Captiva Island, where he escapes each spring to play golf while his emaciated wife lolls poolside, slathered in baby oil, sipping umbrella drinks and grousing about the native staff. It would have been impossible for Louise to let his call go to voicemail. She adores her daddy as none of my daughters do me.

"Hey, Poppo!" she sang. "Having fun?"

A few seconds later, her face burst like a water balloon. She bent over, fanning a hand in front of her face. My first thought was that menopause had struck, but then I realized that Bill had given her bad news. Sarah and Karen dashed to her. I strode over in a manly fashion and reached for the phone. She crouched, clutching it. I wrenched it free. She screamed as if I had ripped out one of her fingernails.

"What the hell was that?" Bill asked.

"Your daughter being melodramatic. What's up?"

"Barbara woke up with chest pains. She's in the hospital for observation. Probably just gas."

"Lovely. That's it?"

"Yep, no big deal."

"Then why the fuck did you ruin our Easter dinner with it?"

"Mal!" Louise screamed.

An overreaction, yes, but only a slight one, when you consider that I have never once stood up to the bully. The girls were just as aghast as Louise was. What had inspired me to do it? To abruptly "grow a pair," as the comedians say? I have no idea. Maybe it's that I'm halfway out the door and no longer care what he thinks of me.

Louise lunged for the phone. I stepped aside like a matador, and she flopped to the Persian carpet. I clicked the call to an abrupt end.

"What's the matter with you?" Louise shouted as the girls helped her to her feet. "My mom's sick and you're telling my father to eff off?"

I shouted back: "I didn't tell him to eff off! I've never told anyone to eff off! In fact, the word 'eff' isn't even in my effing vocabulary!"

I laughed good-naturedly. No one even smiled. The girls

always take their mother's side. A distinct shortage of men around here. If only Archer were alive. I jammed the cordless phone into a deep pocket of my gray flannels and returned to the table. If Louise wanted to call him back, she would have to do it upstairs.

I carved the lamb in silence. I wanted to say: "Goddamn it, your mother is seventy-seven years old and has smoked like a Serbian whore since she was fifteen. Her only exercise is cutting the price tags off Chanel bags and bidding three no-trump. Her diet consists of cucumber, cottage cheese, gin, and lime wedges. Instead of worrying that she might die at any moment, how about thanking your lucky stars she's lasted as long as she has? Because no one deserves it less." I did not say this, of course. Instead, as I served her a juicy slice of meat, I murmured: "Your mom'll be fine, honey. I promise. I'm sorry I was rude to Poppo. I'll call him back and apologize, okay?"

She nodded and, even though her eyes were still wet, found a little smile. I felt a fair amount of shame, not that I had lashed out at her father but that for the ten thousandth time I had sacrificed my masculinity and self-respect on the altar of domestic harmony. If only I were the beast Karen described in her essay! At least then I could hold my head up high.

The house is dark now. There is only the rustling of leaves, the hiss and pop of the hearth, the clink of ice cubes, and the occasional jingle of dear Chuck as he dreams. These hours of solitude are my only true comfort. Soon I will have them whenever I please. Most men would grab as much of their wife's fortune as they could and run for the hills. Not I. Let the girls have the cash. Let them start foundations and build mansions and spoil their kids rotten. I want only enough money to survive. Ah, my idealism! Although buried for years beneath myriad compromises, it is not dead. Its heart still beats.

I am carried back to another night when I was just twenty-one, driving cross-country with a pal—he to check out law schools, I to collect raw experience for my art. That's actually how I saw my mission. My grandiosity was breathtaking. Anyway, one night we stopped at a campsite outside a town in Iowa called Lake Amity. The attendant had already fallen asleep, so we drove our station wagon slowly over the gravel drive, past the admission gate, and up a winding road to a hill overlooking miles of dark countryside. After my pal had fallen asleep, I slipped out for a walk. I was romantic then, about the world and about myself. Gazing up at a flawless yellow moon, I was overwhelmed by the certainty that I was going to be a famous author one day, and, more important than all the possessions my celebrity would bring me, or the comfort for my ego, my fame would allow me to meet, dazzle, and marry the woman of my dreams. Without thinking, I unzipped my pants and began to tug. Like the creative acts of all egoistic youths, mine that night was entirely self-conscious. I saw myself in the loftiest of terms. I was a pagan at prayer, a young genius aspiring to metaphor. With the moon as my goddess and symbol and mirror, I was christening my voyage toward a brilliant future. My friend might have woken up—anyone might have seen me—but I didn't care. There was only my boundless longing and the shy, burnished target of the Midwestern moon.

◆   ◆   ◆   ◆   ◆

"A poet makes a living out of loss." I awoke with this sentence full-born in my head.

◆   ◆   ◆   ◆   ◆

I underestimated the impact of turning fifty. Now that I've had some time to let it sink in, I find it fairly harrowing. No evading it now: I am closer to my death than I am to my birth. I have begun my descent into the cold, dark valley. There's no telling how long it will take. Will I bounce to the bottom with gathering speed like a boulder, or will I enjoy a slow, steady, scenic decline? Who cares but me? The middle-aged feel most deeply the sadism of passing time. The young, even one's own children, go about their blind, eager business. The elderly, having already given up, shrug at our complaints. "What can you do?" they sigh.

With each passing hour, my choices lose import. No one is watching me anymore. My sexual allure daily dwindles. Bones creak. Skin wrinkles and slides. Hairs sprout everywhere but where they are welcome. No one wants to fuck me. Except Death, of course, squatting like a giant, hungry toad in the shadows at the valley's bottom. It frets not the precise hour of its next meal. Why should it? A fresh supply of flesh lands each hour at the brink of its haughty lips.

From the moment we draw first breath, we're merely killing time. Before fifty this is a bad song lyric; after, it is a dire truth. And so each day we craft our own eulogies, preparing ourselves for the first shovelful of soil across the box—unless "soul clap its hands and sing!" Ah, yes, art. Imagination is the only exit. My novel will vanquish death. I will begin writing it on my first morning of freedom. No more booze tonight. I will pay for this. Come, dear Chuck, let us douse the hearth and up to bed. We have the rest of our lives ahead.

◆　◆　◆　◆　◆

This morning, in an effort to extend the holiday weekend, Louise begged Sarah and Karen to play hooky. When they agreed, she asked me to call in sick.

"But the new job numbers are coming in," I improvised.

"Oh, shut up!" she laughed. "Just do it."

As I am vocal about my hatred of hikes ("walks to nowhere"), Louise decided that rather than put her plan to a vote, she would keep it secret. The girls grabbed me by the arms and charmed me all the way to Louise's new Jaguar. I was so tickled by their attention that I didn't even notice their thick shirts, ugly boots, and water bottles. The next thing I knew we were trudging up Hook Mountain.

Because Karen was slowed down by her addiction to carbohydrates, and Louise by her need to say hello to every bee and wildflower, Sarah and I ended up way ahead of them. This suited me just fine, as we had not had a proper heart-to-heart in months. After asking about her academic and social lives (both are "awesome"), I brought up Karen's college essay. I asked whether or not she had read it, and, if so, what she thought of it.

Sarah burst into tears. I was struck dumb, as she is usually so chipper. I eased her down on a rock and asked what was wrong. I am embarrassed to admit this, but I actually thought that she might be crying because she felt that Karen had been unfair to dear old Dad. Not so. Sarah said that the way I treat Mommy absolutely breaks her heart. She loathes my sarcasm even more than Karen and Annie do. (Evidently they have discussed it.) She said that Louise is one of the kindest people on earth and doesn't deserve to be abused like this. And even if she weren't the gentle, loving, and defenseless person she is, didn't I think that her having survived a stroke was reason enough to treat her better?

I longed to tell her the whole heartbreaking truth about our marriage, but I knew that it would make her life an agony between now and when I leave. I want these last months to be as pleasant as possible for everyone. There are few things I dread as much as I do chaos and melodrama.

I pulled Sarah to her feet, and after we had walked for a bit, I explained that children seldom understand the rituals of communication that exist between their parents, and that what looked to her like sarcasm was in fact a private language of humor that began before she was born. I also reminded her that her mom's stroke was never life-threatening and that its only lasting effect was a weakened left leg, which hardly warrants special treatment. I mean, look at her. She's a hiker!

"But if it's not abuse," Sarah countered, "then why is Mommy so nervous around you? Don't you see it? She's scared to death of you, and it's only getting worse."

I countered that not only did I not see it, but I doubted it was even true. Besides, matrimony was a complicated business and that, as unimaginable as it might seem to her, there were ways in which her mom frightened me.

For the next half-hour up the mountain we hardly spoke, although she did mention that Annie and Joshua had moved in together, which she thought only made sense, seeing as how they were going to be inseparable anyway, once "Fisch in a Barrel" started shooting. So Annie was producing the film and no one had bothered to tell me. And now she's paying his rent, as well. Marriage will certainly be next. I suppose it's my punishment for being a sadist. I am disgusted with all three of them right now, truth be told. But it will surely pass, as all feelings do.

◆　◆　◆　◆　◆

Yes, of course, I am short-tempered with Louise, but when I consider the facts in any objective way, I think it is a miracle that I have not lost control and strangled her. Among her many annoying habits are the following, in no particular order: Her voice is piping, her laugh unimaginably wheezy and grating, and her attempts at humor breathtakingly banal. She butchers cliché and idiom. Last week she said, "He thinks he's the greatest thing since spilt milk." She says, "Better safe than never," "Death and taxes wait for no man," "Between a hard rock and a place," and "He ran ramshackle over me." When corrected, she laughs it off, claiming to be dyslexic, which is untrue (and even if it were true, irrelevant), or that it's not her fault that I knocked her up and she was forced to quit college, which is also false. (She used foam with no diaphragm, insisting that it was almost as effective.) She sings to herself continually as she putters around the house looking for surfaces to tell Rosa to dust. She watches soap operas and reads gossip magazines, but, if reminded that they're a brainless waste of time, she says, "That's the whole point." She thinks it's charming to reply to a joke with crossed eyes and a stuck-out tongue. She calls me "baby" all the time, though I have begged her to stop. It's what my mother called me, and it's an erection killer. She ends every single phone call, no matter how fleeting, with "Love you tons!" or "Love you loads!"—the oral equivalent of the smiley face. Whenever she needs to use the bathroom, she pipes "potty time!" When she gets overexcited, which is often, spittle sprays from her mouth, and I am forced to duck for cover. Whenever she leaves the house, even just to stroll the garden, she sticks a yellow note to the refrigerator, informing me of the fact. I have not so much as glanced at a single one of them since the election of Bill Clinton, and I have told her this, but she posts them anyway. Although she is still fit and pretty, her chin is beginning to sprout tiny hairs. They are visible only in direct sunlight, but soon will haunt my days and nights. Worst of all, she is always upbeat and encouraging. Sometimes when I am blue, I would love to hear "Yeah, people are rotten. God is either dead or demented. The world is shit." Not "Don't be sad, baby. It's going to work out. It always does. And even if it doesn't, you have me and the girls." Despite all of the above, everyone finds Louise adorable and sympathetic. The girls can't stop hugging and kissing her. But when I reach out to them, they recoil as though I were covered in weeping sores.

If I believed that my daughters' disdain for me was permanent, I would be standing right now on a railing of the Tappan Zee Bridge, flapping my wings, prepared for take-off. Most of my adult life has been little more than a sustained sacrifice on their behalf. If my only reward for it were their undying scorn, it would mean the world was indeed a vile, unjust place, so why not take a swan dive onto the mainmast of a tugboat? I have faith, however, that once I move out and explain everything, the scales will fall from their eyes, and they will understand me at last. They will appreciate all that I have done for them, and their love will be reborn. Ah, reborn. You see? Happy Easter.

♦ ♦ ♦ ♦ ♦

Two gals talking at the gym today: One said that she had no idea that the other's sister had died and wanted to know how it had happened. Her friend replied: "She was standing on the sidewalk in broad daylight, and a drunk driver jumped the curb. She was thrown through a plate glass window. She was killed instantly." This shook me, not only because the brevity of her answer conveyed the blunt force of tragedy, but also because these same words could be applied to Archer's death. Except it wasn't a car.

A few minutes later, with sweet Archer still on my mind, I spotted a small Latina lifting weights on a distant machine. I am not sure why I noticed her. Her features, hidden in the shade of a baseball cap, were pretty but not terribly refined. Her body was lithe and toned, but that is true of most of the young women who work out at my overpriced club on weekdays afternoons. The most striking thing about her was the way her fuzzy pink gym trunks rode very high on her lean thighs, outlining the contours of her snatch. Because I wasn't subtle in my interest, a male voice whispered in my ear: "She does porn." I turned my head, and there was Archie smiling at me. He had shaved off his curls. His arms were crossed over his barrel chest, showing off his big biceps, still padded with an endearing hint of baby fat.

"You're kidding," I said.

"Nope."

"How do you know?"

"A member recognized her. I overheard him talking to her. She wasn't embarrassed at all."

"What's her name?"

"Veronica Veronique."

"Come on."

"Dude, it's not her real name. Her real name's probably Lucy Diaz or some shit."

He laughed. I sat on a bench and must have looked anxious. He asked what was wrong.

I said, "I'm just trying to digest the fact that when I get home, if I want to, I can sit down at my computer and watch her have sexual intercourse. What a world we live in, eh?"

"Yeah, it's amazing. Ready for your free evaluation yet?"

"No, I—"

"Of course not. I mean, you're doing so great on your own. What's that you're lifting, twelve pounds?"

"Almost twenty."

He snickered and walked off. But it was not obnoxious in the least. In fact, I found it adorable and puckish. It reminded me of my Archer as a toddler. I would ask him if I was his number one daddy, and he would say, "No, you're number four daddy. I want to buy a new daddy." And we would laugh together. If he had grown up to be even half as endearing as this young man, I would have been thrilled.

An hour ago, alone at my desk, I sat for a good ten minutes with Veronica Veronique's name typed into my Google box. It's strange how I betray Louise emotionally in myriad ways, but when it comes to sexual betrayal, even one that is a merely ocular, I am paralyzed with fear. My spotless record of monogamy is a source of great pride for me.

Finally, I hit return and a page of naked photos appeared. I instantly shut it. A minute later, cigarette in hand, I hit it again, and my eyes feasted. Veronica is not your run-of-the-mill slut. She is a shaved, giddy, demented little devil. I took a deep breath, then clicked on her website. Although it is as pink and frilly as a valentine, it showed image after image of her bent into impossible shapes, admitting into her tiny smooth body cocks the size of her forearm. I am no fan of pornography and would normally have grown bored fairly quickly, but I had just seen the girl in the flesh, and it lent an added fascination.

Finally, unable to resist, I clicked on one of her free video samples. A patrolman returns her runaway puppy, and Veronica rewards him with a fierce sucking. I lasted only a few minutes before I ducked into the pool house for a tug. My sex drive has been connubially and pharmaceutically suppressed for so long that it's like a giant captive ape. One of its chains was snapped the day I quit my meds. When the other chain goes, watch out, Nora Woodling!

◆　◆　◆　◆　◆

In the course of a one-hour Chinese lunch on Friday, Nora and I discussed, among other things, the works of Dickens, Chekhov, Tolstoy, Austen, Trollope, Hopkins, Thomas, Yeats, Joyce, Eliot, and Hardy. This morning at breakfast, Louise yammered about her allergies and what Karen should wear to the prom. Someone wise once said: "Marry for conversation; it's the only thing that lasts." Trust me, next time I will.

◆　◆　◆　◆　◆

My prostate has never hurt worse. I imagine free radicals scuttling across my pelvic floor.

◆　◆　◆　◆　◆

The in-laws hosted a brunch today in Karen's honor. Bastard Bill was in high spirits. The melanoma farm he calls a nose is still crimson and peeling from the links on Captiva. Babs looked even browner and scrawnier than usual. The doctor said that her chest pains were, indeed, the result of acute indigestion, and that as long as she curbed her alcohol intake and continued to take Lipitor, Cozaar, Atenolol, Plavix, and Imdur, she ought to be fit as a fiddle until her next bypass. We all toasted the happy prognosis, but inwardly I brooded.

I have been looking forward to her death for years now. She is impossibly self-centered and callous. Why Louise dotes on her is beyond my comprehension, unless it is the mere devotion of a hostage to her captor.

An awkward moment came when Bill said he and Babs had decided that for our anniversary they would give us something we would never give ourselves: "A first-class all-expenses-paid Caribbean cruise! You set sail in September." The girls cheered with excitement. Louise turned to me, eyes blossoming with joy and hope. My eyes, on the other hand.... Well, any sentient being would have seen that I was stricken with horror.

"Wow, so generous," I whimpered. "I can't thank you enough. Unfortunately, I work for a living."

Louise's face sagged.

Karen shook her head at me as though I had just sung the praises of kitten rape.

"To hell with that," Bill laughed. "Want me to call Cal myself? I'd be happy to."

"Please don't. I have a hunch the chairman of the company has more important things to do than worry about my vacations. When the date gets closer, I'll talk to Doug and see if he can spare me. How's that?"

Louise jabbed silently at her quiche.

Karen and Sarah exchanged dark, furtive glances.

Later, I walked the grounds alone, gazing out at the old stables, desperately craving a cigarette, when Bastard Bill came up behind me, puffing a cigar. I have never understood why Louise tolerates his smoking and yet despises mine so much.

Bill blew at the sky, "I don't want to hear another word about what a hard-ass I am."

"What do you mean?

"Lou-Lou didn't tell you?"

"Maybe she did, and I forgot."

"I put a call in."

"Could you be more specific?"

"To Brown."

He laughed when he saw my shocked face.

"What, you thought Karen made it in all by herself? With those rotten scores? Not in a million years."

"You didn't tell her, I hope."

"Hell no. Although she'll probably figure it out when she sees my name go up on the new library." He laughed again, when he saw my reaction. "Jesus, Mal! I'm kidding. Lighten up. When did you get so god-damn serious?"

◆ ◆ ◆ ◆ ◆

This morning, walking down the halls of the mental-health clinic, I suddenly realized why I felt sick to my stomach. Since Yale, I had worked only two jobs. In order to land the first, as a housekeeper, I had been required to answer just one simple question: "With your education, why the hell do you want to be a housekeeper?" To land the second, at the magazine, I attended a Southampton cocktail party and pretended to love Ronald Reagan. In other words, this was my first real job interview.

The office of the County Suicide Help Line is a bland rectangular room with three carrels on each side. When I walked in, two of the staff were chatting on their phones, while three others scrolled on their laptops. One carrel was empty. If I got the job, it would certainly be mine. A red-haired giantess jumped up to greet me. I immediately wished I had stopped in the men's room. My brow was moist and my prostate burned for an imaginary pee.

The giantess introduced herself as Peg Rubo, then walked me to the back of the room, just as Henry Glover, the program director, emerged from his office with another applicant—a stone-faced Asian kid who looked about half my age. As he passed by me, he slipped on a face mask, protecting himself, no doubt, against airborne pathogens. A few of the staff noticed and chuckled. The kid was toast.

Glover ushered me into his office. Thank God, he was not intimidating in the least. Black and bald with a mustache, he leaned back in his chair and asked me nothing but breezy, superficial questions, and he couldn't have seemed less interested in my answers. I thought he might fall asleep. He only perked up when I told him that I had taken early retirement from *Investors Monthly* because I wanted to write a novel.

"Oh, the arty type. You related to Edgar Allan?"

"Distant cousin," I lied.

"Neat. Got a title yet? For your book?"

"*The Dead of Spring*," I replied, having no idea where it came from.

"I like it. What's it about?"

"Sorry, I live by Goethe's dictum: 'Poet—don't talk.'"

"Secretive."

"Just prudent. Talking lets the air out of the balloon. Papa Hemingway put it best: 'The stories you tell, you never write.'"

"So why do you wanna work here?"

"I don't believe any human being, not even a writer, should live in isolation. We're social animals by nature. When I disconnect from my community, I feel unmoored."

"Huh."

"I think Obama's right. Public service ought to be a top priority for every American."

He flashed a cocky smile. "I'm a Republican."

Mine was just as cocky as I lied again: "Me too. But even a broken clock's right twice a day."

Oh, we enjoyed a smug chuckle over that one. I really disliked the creep, but I left feeling confident that the gig was mine. Only when I stepped out into a cool breeze did I notice that the front of my shirt was drenched with sweat. Had he noticed? Luckily, I had kept my blazer buttoned.

◆　◆　◆　◆　◆

The end of Eva: Each choice we make alters the course of our lives, and yet, because we never know what would have happened if we had chosen otherwise, we never know if we have chosen wisely. No means of comparison. We improvise on air. It ought to drive us insane or maybe even liberate us, but instead we are plagued by regret and futile speculation.

Had I kept quiet when I spotted Louise running toward the Notre Dame cathedral, she would have ducked inside and never been the wiser. Instead, I called out her name. A dead stop, a swish of blond hair, and she saw me. She cried out and flew to me with her long, skinny arms outstretched. Before I could speak, she peppered me with lipless kisses and heartfelt apologies. Somehow she'd gotten it into her head that we were meeting Sunday instead of Saturday. When she'd realized her mistake, she'd run all the way from the Ritz. I glanced at Eva. No emotion in her dark blue eyes. The only hint of distress was the faint blush seeping into her cheeks.

Over the years, I've asked myself why I yelled out Louise's name when it would have been so much easier to hold my tongue. If someone had asked me at the time, I would have said that it was because no matter how deeply I was smitten by Eva, I had known her for a mere few hours, and she lived in fucking Oslo. What if she was not the divine being I believed her to be, or what if she was, but geography spelled our doom? What if she had been unwilling to move to New York? Today I believe the truth is far simpler: At the instant I called Louise's name, I valued, more highly than love and happiness, a hot shower and a steak.

When Louise saw Eva for the first time, she studied her gorgeous face, luscious tits, tiny waist, and ripe thighs. That's when it dawned on her that our botched rendezvous hadn't been as torturous for me as it had been for her.

"This is Eva Birkeland," I said. "From Norway."

Louise oversmiled. "No way!"

"They're not all blond, you know."

Eva and I smiled at our private joke.

"Time to feed my starving artist." Louise grabbed my arm. "Come with us, Eva. Please? My treat."

"Oh, no," she said, "my train leaves soon. I must go now." She met my eyes. "Malcolm, I'm so happy you found your friend. I would have felt terrible, leaving you all by yourself in a big, lonely city."

I hugged the sublime girl. What a rotten day she had had. Rejected first by her pen pal and now by me. She deserved far better. Louise studied our hug, her cramped patrician brain struggling to fathom how we could have grown so intimate so quickly.

I would be rewriting history if I did not confess that the next twelve hours were among the most pleasurable of my young life. Twenty minutes on a clean, white toilet, a long steamy shower and shave, filet mignon wheeled in by a snooty bellman. After dinner, a laundress whisked away every filthy stitch of my clothing, leaving me dressed only in a sumptuous hotel robe. Minutes later, Louise set aside her champagne flute, fell to her knees, opened my robe, and performed the sort of worshipful fellatio that up until then I had thought the stuff only of fantasy.

♦   ♦   ♦   ♦   ♦

"At leaving even the most unpleasant people
And places, one keeps looking at the steeple."
—Lord Byron

♦   ♦   ♦   ♦   ♦

Idea for a short story: Identical twin males marry lovely women and have three happy kids. One twin is monogamous; the other cheats every chance he gets. The first dies of rectal cancer at fifty; the second lives to be eighty-five. There's definitely something there.

♦   ♦   ♦   ♦   ♦

Today Nora and I wandered into an upscale grill whose name already eludes me. The sort of place where, before the economy staggered, you needed a reservation, but now you get seated pretty quickly. Nora took off her jacket and, for the first time, was not wearing a prudish cotton blouse buttoned all the way to her chin, but something soft and silky that showed an inch of bra on both sides and a tiny swell of cleavage. I'm not sure why. Maybe because the week of my departure is now set in stone.

   As usual, we talked mostly about books. I explained that as a young man I had read in a methodical way—moving through all of Proust, for example, or Dostoevsky or Zola—but that since leaving the magazine I had made a conscious choice to free myself up. I read now in a more scattershot way, gathering a diverse pile of library books each morning, sampling them at random, and moving on to the next book whenever I grow restless.

"I'm not sure if this is a step forward," I concluded, "or if I'm suffering from some sort of adult-onset Attention Deficit Disorder."

She laughed and said that the haphazard way I'm reading is actually wonderful and might lead me to authors and books I would never have known existed. She said that I must try not to be so hard on myself, that self-criticism cripples the spirit and thwarts the imagination. She spoke from experience, she said, because one of the side effects of her Catholic education is a tendency toward perfectionism, which renders her incapable of writing even one decent line of verse. Moved, I took her slender hands and kissed them. She enjoyed it momentarily, but then removed them.

"Please don't do that again," she whispered, her green eyes growing moist.

"I'm sorry. It's hard to hold back."

Later, I asked her if she had a favorite poem. She said that she always has one, but it changes every few months.

"And your current one is?"

"'Howl' by Allen Ginsberg."

"You just surprised me."

"I did? Why?"

"I expected something more traditional and romantic. Any more surprises?"

I am not sure what I expected to hear. Maybe I was just being flirtatious.

"Yes. I'm a virgin," she said.

She watched me, smiling with a hint of hauteur, as the news sank in.

"Disappointed?" she asked.

"Stunned. Do you mind if I ask why?"

"Not at all. I've only been in love twice. The first with a man who was happily married. The second was a homosexual. Both made physical intimacy impossible."

"Don't you mean *unethical*?"

Her eyes bulged as though to draw a distinction between the two were unthinkable. Then, certain that I must be joking, she released a trill of shy, embarrassed laughter.

I am sure that a good psychologist would have a field day with what I am about to confess, but I am happy that Nora is a virgin. I can think of no better way to restart my sex life than with a woman who is just commencing hers.

◆　◆　◆　◆　◆

Dear Girls, on this lonely night, I'm thinking about a Sherwood Anderson story I read when I was a teenager. I forget the title, but it's about a young farmer, married with kids, who can't bear the strain and drudgery of his life one minute longer. In the dead of a moonless night, he bolts across the farmyard with only the clothes on his back. He runs over acres and acres of plowed fields into utter darkness. We're in his head the whole time, as he recalls the tedious misery that's inspired his rash escape. He has no idea where he's going, but anything is better than this. At the edge of his land, he stops, hands on his knees, gasping for air. He wheels around, gazing back at the tiny, flickering light of his homestead. He imagines his wife and children sleeping inside, bundled in shadows, trusting that when they wake he'll be there, providing and protecting. He drops his head and slowly, slowly, slowly, walks home.

At least that's how I remember it.

When I first read the story, I thought it was a domestic love poem, a paean to marital fidelity. The author understood that everyone resents, at times, the ties that bind us to our spouses and children, but only a fool severs them, because they lend our lives its most precious meaning. Only years later did I learn that in real life Sherwood Anderson, after suffering a nervous breakdown, abandoned his wife and three small children to pursue his literary career. I was appalled by this and wondered if I had entirely misread the story. Was I meant to be inspired by the courage of the young farmer when he turned for home or to lament his cowardice? Incredibly, Anderson's abandonment of his family was hailed by his disciples as proof of his artistic dedication, but the way I see it no artist is a hero when his work is born of cruelty and betrayal.

Apollo and Dionysus are often said to clash in the imagination of the artist, but I maintain that the two fight each other only in those of limited talent. In the truly brilliant, they live in perfect accord, even sharing a common dominatrix: the all-powerful Hestia, goddess of hearth and home. (I picture her as beautiful and buxom, but perpetually pissed off, scowling and waving a rolling pin.) The Greeks understood the titanic pull of domestic responsibility. That's why the first and last offering at all of their religious ceremonies was to Hestia.

My heart aches for those, like me, whose talents lie buried beneath a pile of dirty dishes or an avalanche of toddler kisses. We're the true heroes of the artistic world, not the Tolstoys and Picassos who create masterworks but treat their loved ones worse than shit. Perhaps, my darling girls, you won't understand what I've sacrificed for you until you are married yourself, sitting home alone at night with your babies, while your husbands are out in the world pursuing their stupid, selfish dreams.

◆ ◆ ◆ ◆ ◆

Dinner at the City Cafe with Trey and Li Ming Montgomery. At one point, I launched a comic ode to the curative properties of ginger, which made everyone laugh, until it became clear that it was, in fact, a parody of Li Ming's passion for all things healing and holistic. Trey rubbed his wife's back and offered comforting words as she cried. Louise stammered an apology. I was mortified. I seem to have lost my ability to gauge how people will respond to my humor. I apologized, too, of course, insisting that it was all meant in good fun. Li Ming said it was okay and that she was just hormonal, but no one bought it. The evening had been permanently altered. Louise really let me have it, driving home. I didn't even bother to defend myself.

◆ ◆ ◆ ◆ ◆

Read "Howl" many times last night and this morning. An unruly but remarkable work that makes repeated mention of the mental hospital in Rockland where my father stayed the winter before he hanged himself. It resonates powerfully with me. There is a line about those "who cut their wrists three times successively unsuccessfully, gave up and were forced to open antiques stores where they thought they were growing old and cried." It makes me wonder whether Nora has tried to kill herself before. Or maybe Rhodes has. Is he the gay man with whom Nora was once in love? There's so much about her I don't know, but I must not force it. I must let the bud open naturally.

I have the idea in my head that it would be a wonderful gift to Nora if I memorized "Howl" and recited it to her one day while she was lying in my arms. Or even sooner. Sadly, it's six pages long, and I lack the brain cells. I suppose I could manage the first hundred lines or so. Or maybe the last hundred. The lines about Rockland. I had always thought the poem was about mental illness, but it's actually about what it means to be creative in the United States. A thin line.

◆   ◆   ◆   ◆   ◆

A demented stranger on the train today explained that flu season was created by the government to cull the population of the Third World, bring windfall profits to the manufacturers of anti-virals, and to render our citizenry docile with terror. I told him that it was a pretty ingenious plan and that I expected nothing less from a Harvard man like Obama. That shut him up pretty fast!

I wonder if there is a short story to be written about one of these modern types who see conspiracy everywhere. The more helpless the hero feels in his own puny life, the grander the conspiracies he imagines. In the final scene, he squats naked in a hole in his backyard, certain that his house is surrounded by shock troops. When he hears his name being called, he knows all is lost. He bravely stands, arms raised, ready to be shot through the heart. There staring at him is his neighbor's fatherless boy, come to fetch a baseball that flew over the fence. Our hero rises. Wakes from his delirium. Plays

catch with the kid. Unofficially adopts him. Something like
that. Where do I get these ideas?

◆　◆　◆　◆　◆

Henry Glover just called and hired me for the suicide help
line. My hours are nine to five Tuesdays and Thursdays. The
pay is twenty dollars an hour. Although much of what I said
during the interview was baloney, I meant what I said about
how I feel unmoored without a connection to my community.
I am thrilled to be moored again, even if only in this limited
way. The only snag will be that if Louise ever wants to ride
into the city with me on a day when I am working at the help
line, I will be forced to come down with a sudden illness.

◆　◆　◆　◆　◆

Writing about Eva has stirred up so many memories that I
was inspired to Google her just now. First time ever. She's
the executive director of a Norwegian non-profit working to
secure loose nukes. I was ready to run an image search when
my mouse finger froze. Did I really want to see her as she looks
today? Cropped gray hair, jowls, pendulous breasts? Based on
what I learned at my last high school reunion, any nightmare
is possible. Or maybe she's still a beauty, as well preserved as I
am. The Internet is a fearsome thing. Never in human history
have cherished memories been so vulnerable to destruction.
Reality lies crouched, just a few mouse clicks away. On the
other hand, clinging to the past, for whatever reason, reflects
a weakness of character, doesn't it? Nostalgia of any kind is a
gutless avoidance of the only thing that matters: the spiritual
preparation for death.

♦ ♦ ♦ ♦ ♦

Time to start looking for my own place. I've decided to furnish it in a spare modern way. I am sick of drawers that do not close, gleaming tables on which no uncoastered glass can ever be laid, and ancient leather chairs that powder my ass brown. It would surprise Louise to know this, but I have come to hate her family heirlooms. Lately I crave the contemporary in all things. Nora might feel differently, so I must be prepared to compromise on this. And on everything else, I suppose. I wonder if she is any good at compromise. I doubt many adult virgins are.

♦ ♦ ♦ ♦ ♦

Louise and Annie talked on the phone tonight, while I stood outside the ajar bedroom door, eavesdropping as best I could. Louise spoke mostly in whispers. When I sensed the call was winding down, I barged in with a smile, grabbed the phone, and sang "My turn!" Louise glared at me as though this were an outrageous intrusion into our daughter's life. I plopped down on the chaise and asked Annie how "Fisch in a Barrel" was going. She was surprised that I knew her secret, but she recovered quickly and said that pre-production had just begun and was going brilliantly. Joshua is an incredible mentor, she claimed. He was teaching her how to make a dollar go a very long way.

"Necessity is the mother of invention," I proclaimed.

"It sure is."

"Well, I just want to say I'm sorry I've been so unfair to him. My feelings were hurt because you said I was a born editor. Maybe I'm a delusional old fool, but I think I still have a novel or two in me yet."

I waited for her to tell me that I was not a delusional old fool, but she did not.

So there it was, writ large.

One minute I'm the apple of my daughter's eye and the next I'm a fucking joke.

"Apology accepted?" I croaked.

"Sure, Daddy."

I tossed the phone and walked out.

◆ ◆ ◆ ◆ ◆

First day of training. According to Big Peg Rubo, two thirds of the legitimate calls that the help line receives are from people looking for free psychotherapy. This is the easiest part of the job, because all I have to do is get a basic read on their problems and then refer them to a local clinic. The other third are from people who are either on the verge of self-slaughter or genuinely fear themselves to be. The first thing you do is put them at ease, slow them down, and make a human connection. They suggest "active listening," a technique whereby you parrot whatever the person says. It makes people feel "heard." The quotation marks are not mine. This is how they say it. Peg says active listening can also work wonders outside the office.

Once the caller is relaxed, inquire as to his psychiatric history. Has he attempted suicide before? How does he plan to do it this time? Listen carefully in order to assess the likelihood that he will actually follow through. Key questions: Are there drugs and alcohol involved? Any signs of undiagnosed mental illness? Is the caller alone? Does he have the means on hand to kill himself? Does he have a support system—friends, family, clergyman, shrink? If we believe that a suicide attempt might be imminent, we signal a co-worker to call rescue emergency services. Once help has arrived and the call is concluded, you must take an honest self-inventory and ask yourself if you are okay to keep working. Do you need a few minutes alone? If you become anxious or depressed later, is there someone at home you can talk to?

So that the state knows its tax dollars are being spent wisely, we're asked to keep a written record of each call. If you get a name, great; if not, just write "Anonymous." There are no requirements as to length. Most reports are fairly succinct, but some go on and on and on. One rule, however, is strictly enforced: Notes must be jotted down on paper and then typed into the computer later. Typing while a caller is on the line is a gigantic no-no. Our customers are exquisitely sensitive. The sound of a clicking keyboard could send them right out the window.

While Big Peg briefed me, she ate egg salad on a pumpernickel bagel. With each bite, the egg oozed out everywhere. She wiped away the excess with a mannish finger and sucked it clean. Peg is a hulking lass, but her face is pretty and so is her thick rusty hair and toothy smile. She wore a yellow dress that worked magic on me. Her big, bare, tanned legs are flecked with golden hairs. God bless the spring! I can't remember my last public erection—probably back in junior high—but today, as I imagined Peg stark naked and pretzeled into the same positions as Veronica Veronique, my crotch went crazy. A ferret in a sack. I have been pent up for far too long. I hope that Nora is enough to satisfy me. I have a hunch she will prove to be either a voracious lover or an absolute ice sculpture. How sad it will be if I am forced to leave her because we are incompatible between the sheets.

◆ ◆ ◆ ◆ ◆

Louise's old pals from the lecture series invited us over tonight for take-out vegan and face-time with their infant gift from God. Louise had told me all about Miles Alan Gardner, describing him as "scrumptious," but since I know she would never describe a baby in terms less charitable than these, I feared the worst. Sure enough, the kid is an unremarkable lump of cells. Big head, no chin, elephant ears, tiny eyes, and an excess of drool. Naturally the Gardners have no idea that he is a fright, because this would require a level of objectivity beyond the reach of new parents, but what was Louise's excuse? Tonight she did not call him "scrumptious." She switched to "divine." Just to amuse myself, I poked the nipper where his chin should have been and said, "Aw, look at that smile. It's positively diabolical."

I had thought Ellie's body had snapped back pretty well until I saw the hundred framed photographs of her and Greg that adorn every horizontal surface (and one vertical one: a snapshot-filled wall divider). It turns out she is still just a caricature of her former self. Before Greg seeded her, she was an absolute doll. A slim-hipped chew toy with the smile of a toothpaste model. At one point, not five feet from me, she pulled up her blouse, yanked down her bra, and dumped a handful of nipple into Miles's snapping jaws. It was not an image I will be able to banish anytime soon.

After dinner, I sipped coffee with Greg on the brick patio (stained with cat pee) and asked if I might pick his brain for a few minutes about New York City real estate. He said that Rockland and Westchester counties were his bailiwick, but if he could be of help, sure, fire away. I asked him where all the starving artists live these days. In the 1980s it was the

East Village, Alphabet City, and the Lower East Side, but now where? Brooklyn, right? Which neighborhood?

"Why do you want to know?" he asked, brow furrowing.

"A friend of mine's leaving his wife."

Suddenly Louise, who I had no idea was even outside, plopped down next to Greg.

"Who?" she asked with concern.

My mind went blank and my mouth dry.

"Tom Feldsher," I blurted. "He's leaving Cindy."

"Oh no!"

"I thought I told you."

"Is it because of that Juliet girl?"

"Hacker? Yes. I mean, well, no. He's still seeing her, but she's not the reason they're divorcing. He was a painter in college, and he wants to get back to it."

Louise and Greg laughed in unison.

"What's so funny?" I could feel my face prickling. "He just took the job at the magazine to pay the bills after Tia was born. She's away at boarding school. He's bored with the marriage. They have plenty of dough since his mother died. It's the perfect time to start over and go back to his first love."

"That is such bullcrap," Louise said. "It isn't enough that he cheats on her, now he's going to run off and play starving artist? Who does he think he is, Paul Gauguin?"

"I've got to agree with your better half, Mal," Greg said. "Sounds pretty self-indulgent to me."

"I'll say." Ellie joined us, dabbing curd off her shirt. "Totally narcissistic."

The thought of these three passing judgment on my friend and his imaginary liberation absolutely galled me.

I said, "What if, for argument's sake, Tom happens to be

genuinely brilliant with an important contribution to make
to our culture? Would that make any difference to you?"

A robust chorus of "No!" was followed by Louise saying,
"Anyway, he's not brilliant."

"Oh, really?"

"Brilliant artists don't work in publishing for fifteen years
and then wake up one day and say, 'Hold on a minute, what
am I doing? I'm the next Picasso! I better buy some paints and
move to Williamsburg!'"

"Lou, you're hilarious," Greg said.

"Were you an actress in high school?" Ellie asked.

I felt like punching them all. I bit into the side of my coffee
cup so I wouldn't say something I'd regret. I'd have paid a
thousand dollars for a cigarette.

"Anyway, back to your original question, Greg said. "A
cool, hip area is DUMBO. 'Down Under Manhattan Bridge
Overpass.'"

"Sure."

"And then there's Washington Heights—now called
Hudson Heights—but these days it's mostly families moving in. I'd say your friend's best bet is between Columbia
University and Harlem. It doesn't have a name yet. A buddy
of mine calls it the Upper Upper West Side."

Ellie and Louise laughed.

"A real estate agent thought of that?" I deadpanned. "It's
so clever."

My tone was off. Too nasty. It created tension. We left
soon thereafter. Driving home, I was unable to shake the feeling that I, not Tom, had been the evening's laughingstock.
Louise knew something was wrong.

"What is it, sweetheart?" she asked softly, with real
sympathy.

"Nothing. I just didn't like the way everybody ganged up on Tom."

"What do you care?"

"We're pals."

"But when we saw him on the train, you were furious he was cheating on Cindy."

"I got over it. He told Cindy about it. And, guess what, she was fine with it. She's even fine with the fact that he's moving out."

"Fine in what way?"

"She said, 'I'd rather lose you, knowing that you're happy, than keep you, knowing that you're unhappy, living a lie.'"

"I don't buy it. No woman thinks like that."

"Well, I'm afraid that says more about you than it does about her. She's truly selfless."

We settled into silence. I turned on classical music. I hoped she was thinking about what I had just said and wondering whether she would be as noble as Cindy under similar circumstances, but when I looked over at her, she was moving her head to the symphony. As usual, she wasn't thinking about a thing.

♦ ♦ ♦ ♦ ♦

Finished my final day of observation. Thursday I take my first suicide call. Big Peg says baptism by fire is always best.

♦ ♦ ♦ ♦ ♦

Flaubert: "You have to read fifteen hundred books in order to write one."

✦ ✦ ✦ ✦ ✦

Voltaire: "Optimism is the madness of insisting that all is well when we are miserable."

✦ ✦ ✦ ✦ ✦

Henry James's cousin once wrote to him: "The remote possibility of the best thing is always better than a clear certainty of the second-best thing." No Utopian, I would be more than happy to settle for the second-best thing. Or even the third. My marriage is far from even that.

✦ ✦ ✦ ✦ ✦

I picked up the phone and heard a man blubbering something I could not make out.

"Calm down, sir," I said. "I can't understand a word you're saying."

The caller cried, "Sir? I'm female!"

I was astonished. Her voice was deeper than mine. I wondered if this was some sort of practical joke. It was, after all, my first solo call. What better time to haze me? I looked around. None of my co-workers was grinning, biting his lip, or sputtering into his hands. I started over. Everything I'd been taught instantly flew out the window.

"I'm sorry. Truly. Please tell me what's wrong. Do you really want to kill yourself?"

"Yes, yes!" she screamed, and then she unloaded a quart of snot into a tissue.

This was no joke.

Big Peg rolled her chair close and whispered in my ear:

"Don't discuss suicide yet. Get to know him."

I covered the receiver and whispered back: "It's not a him.
It's a her. With a voice like a bass drum."

Everyone laughed. I glared at them. Peg dug her thumbs
into my neck muscles, eased me back in my chair, and
instructed me to breathe. When she gave me the go-ahead,
I started over, calmly asking the caller to tell me more about
the situation. Her story took a full half-hour. She was, by
her own admission, a fat, ugly French horn player who, after
a cancelled gig, found herself alone in a hotel room on a
glorious May morning, gazing out the window at a plaza filled
with skinny, happy people, and all she could think about was
gobbling some pills and going to sleep forever.

The more she talked, the more apparent it became to me
that, although she was miserable (for good reason), she didn't
really want to die, and so I asked her about the things that had
made her happy in the past. She told me about her musical
studies, family vacations, and the good old days when she was
popular and pretty, back when she was in diapers.

Peg, sensing that I was in control, passed me a note that
said, "How long have you been doing this?"

I asked the caller: "How long have you been doing this?"

When Peg flinched, I realized it had been a sweet
compliment meant for me, not a question for the caller.

"Doing what?" the caller asked, bewildered.

"Uhhh...being your own worst enemy."

"A long time," she squeaked. "A real long time."

She agreed to get some psychiatric help, and when I hung
up, everyone applauded. A happy ending!

◆ ◆ ◆ ◆ ◆

Only two other interesting calls. The first was from a sixteen-year-old brat named Arvin, whose psychiatric résumé included trying to bludgeon his mother to death when she grounded him. (He confided this freely, even a tad proudly.) Now he is in despair because he's knocked up his thirty-two-year-old meth-addicted girlfriend. Suicide is the only way out, he insisted. I told him not to be ridiculous and that I would be happy to get him a free psychiatrist, but then I whispered: "If you ask me, what you really need is a good abortionist." He was silent for a second, then laughed and hung up. A little plain talk goes a long way.

The second was from an Adult Protective Services worker named Stuart, asking that a mobile crisis team be rushed to a home in West Haverstraw. The husband is ninety-three and the wife ninety-two. At least once a month, she washes down her pills with peach schnapps and beats the shit out of him with her "old-fashioned wooden leg." (I imagined it wearing a saddle shoe.) Today, things took a turn for the worse when she flattened his nose. The old man called Stuart, blubbering through blood and cartilage that he had had enough and was going to shoot them both. As I put in the request, I could not help but reflect that many more marriages would end this way if both spouses lived to be ninety.

♦   ♦   ♦   ♦   ♦

I think what Big Peg told me during training is correct, that when a caller leads with "I'm going to kill myself," he is seldom serious. She says the ones you have to watch out for are the callers who are either grimly monotone (as though they were calling from the bottom of a deep, dry well) or crazily upbeat and chipper. The vast majority of today's callers were of neither type. They were mostly just lonely people looking for someone to talk at. It's hard not to think that if they listened occasionally, they might not be so lonely. My approach was to let them yammer to their hearts' content while I skimmed a book or magazine and repeated back to them what they had just said. Most talked themselves out in twenty minutes or so, felt better, thanked me profusely, and hung up. The ones who don't feel better, I referred to a shrink.

♦ ♦ ♦ ♦ ♦

The owner of Melody Sandwich, no doubt remembering my chat with Starla's double, eyed me with suspicion as I stepped to the counter. What did he think I was going to do? Reach over the plastic screen, grab a stack of Provolone, and dash for the door? Just to spite him, I tipped the counter girl five dollars on my way out. Her eyes nearly popped out of her head.

Arriving at Bryant Park a full fifteen minutes early, I went off in search of a cigarette. I looked everywhere, but did not spot a single smoker. It's staggering, really, when you consider how cruel and rotten life is, that so many people have been seduced by the longevity lobby. Finally, I spotted a tense woman, walking in tight circles, puffing away like a tardy teenager behind the school. I was not surprised she wanted the cigarette over with. She was a Muslim. Head-scarf and everything. Predictably, she was more than happy to share her poison with me, but no sooner had I blown the first puff skyward than I saw Nora walking toward me, smiling up at the very same sky as though it were a gift that God had wrapped in blue especially for her. I tossed my cigarette, but I was a second too late.

The ensuing lecture I received on the twin evils of smoking and littering was delivered with such adorable seriousness that I could hardly wipe the smile off my face. When Nora was finished, I handed her a tuna fish sandwich, cole slaw, and mineral water. When she saw that I was eating a salami sub and chips, she launched another lecture, on nitrites and cholesterol. She reminded me of a prairie schoolmarm— the pretty kind from the black-and-white movies, whom the students adore and the new doctor in town woos and weds. (In the 1970s version, she is raped by a motorcycle gang.)

After lunch, in lieu of dessert, I recited from memory the last twenty-fives lines from "Howl." She said that it was one of the sweetest things anyone had ever done for her. I replied that I found that surprising, because she is so lovable I would have thought sweet things had been done for her daily since the moment of her birth. Her brow clouded over and she said that it was quite the opposite, that as a child she had been severely abused. I felt a surge of alarm and protectiveness. I asked her how and by whom.

"Not yet," she whispered. "Maybe someday."

As we walked out of the park, she said that, inspired by her newfound respect for Ginsberg, she had picked up a novel by Charles Bukowski. Unfortunately, she could not make it out of the first chapter, not because it lacked artistry (in fact she was surprised at what a deft and charming storyteller he is) but because his descriptions of sex were simply too repugnant. She said that as much as she would like to broaden her literary tastes, there are certain places that she cannot bear to go, and one of them is into sagging beds with soiled sheets. I told her that I was the same way, that I sought out literature not to have my face jammed into the mud, but to be lifted into the arms of angels. She liked that. So did I.

She asked what I was reading these days and I listed for her a dozen of my recent samplings. Mostly French. I mentioned the letters of Flaubert, and how inspired I was by his work ethic, even though it bordered on monomania. George Sand used to beg him to take an occasional walk, and he'd tell her to butt out.

"It shows," Nora replied. "I know he's supposed to be a genius, but when I read *Madame Bovary*, every word is so perfect, I feel like opening a window and letting in some fresh air."

What a joy it was to hear a woman say something like this. Yes, Nora is gorgeous and her body is superb, but when I fantasize about making love to her it is the thought of all that intelligence and erudition squirming beneath me that makes me dizzy with desire. My only fear is that the reason she has been able to remain a virgin for so long is that she is not sensual by nature, and that I will be the only one of us transported by our lovemaking. There are few lonelier feelings than this, and yet, if I am forced to settle for it, I will.

Walking back, Nora opened up about her private life. After work each day, she takes the subway to the YWCA where she swims, lifts weights, and practices yoga. Then she picks up a salad at the Koreans' and heads home. Her landlady is a stooped widow who lets her a single room in return for five hundred dollars a month and the right to dispirit her with daily racist diatribes. Nora owns no TV, stereo, or computer. At night, she reads great literature and occasionally scribbles a few lines of verse. Over the long, lonely years, she has filled dozens of notebooks with these stabs at poetry.

"But I doubt I'll ever show them to anyone," she said. "It's sheer torture for me, yes, torture, to write them. It's so painful I can barely stand it. The thought of showing them to anyone makes me physically ill."

I told her that I keep a journal, my first since my marriage. I opened my briefcase and showed it to her.

"What do you write about?" she asked.

"Lately I find it hard work to write about anything other than you."

She grinned like a happy elf.

If Nora Ann Woodling were a character in a novel, I would assume that she was profoundly eccentric, if not flat-out crazy, and that her staunch defense of her maidenhead is simply a defense against living and loving, but knowing her as I do, I do not believe this to be the case. I think she is a rare spirit who lives on a higher plane than the rest of us. It is imperative that rather than drag her down to my reality, I elevate myself to hers. Anything else would be criminal.

I'm going to ask her to help me find a place to live. Considering that it will almost certainly be the apartment in which she loses her virginity, I can't imagine she'll refuse me. I suppose it's possible that the big event will occur in a luxury hotel suite, if that's how she wants it. I don't particularly care, just so long as it all goes smoothly. I have never made love to a virgin before. Who can forget the gruesome scene in *The Bell Jar* when the Sylvia Plath character loses her virginity and bleeds so profusely that she is rushed to the hospital for stitches? Please, God, don't let that happen to Nora. Chuck is barking at the French doors. He smells a raccoon, possum, or skunk. Just once, I'd love to set him free and see what kind of damage he could do.

♦ ♦ ♦ ♦ ♦

Cocktails at Bing and Fiona's. About eight couples were there, including a Sri Lankan jewelry designer and her historian husband, who bored us to tears with talk of his new book on the Tamil Tigers. When Louise looked confused, I whispered in her ear that they were a baseball team. I was relieved that she didn't believe me. Everything went swimmingly until Tess Bremer, more than tipsy, noticed me at the French doors, gazing up at the night sky. I was thinking about Nora, of course. Tess could not keep her curiosity to herself.

"Hey, get a load of your husband!" she hollered at Louise.

Everyone stopped talking.

"Like the cat that ate the canary," she said, pointing at me. "What the heck does he have to be so happy about?"

"It's an act," Bing snorted. "He's never happy."

"Oh, that's not true," Louise said, a bit defensively.

"No, honey, he's right," I said. "I'm well on my way to curmudgeonhood."

"You're already there," Bing said.

I countered: "No, to officially classify, I believe you've got to be over fifty-five."

"Since when?" Bing walked closer, squinting queerly. "Hey, you do look happy. Did you get an eye-lift or something?"

"I know what it is!" Tess cried. "You have a girlfriend, don't you?"

The best way to quell a suspicion is to surrender to it. Stick your head directly into the lion's mouth, and it usually slinks away.

"You guessed it," I said with a casual shrug. "Fiona, tell everyone what a spectacular lover I am."

Everyone except Bing laughed.

On the way home, Louise asked me if Tess had been right.

"What do you mean?"

"Are you having an affair?"

"With Fiona? She's twice my size and smells like sour milk."

"With someone else."

"Oh, please."

"Yes or no?"

"No!"

"You swear?"

"On the lives of our daughters."

"Don't say that."

"Why not, if it's true?"

Convinced now that she was my one and only, she moved closer, and, as soon as we were inside, reached for my zipper. I had no choice but to comply. I was exhausted and a little drunk, so I needed some outside help. While she fellated me, I imagined Nora walking into the 42nd Street library. I look up from my book and our eyes meet. She gestures with her head for me to follow. When I find her in the stacks, she has already kicked off her loafers and dropped her skirt and pantyhose to the floor. From the waist up, she is fully dressed from work—high-collared blouse and tweed blazer. From the waist down, she is naked—lean thighs, well-groomed snatch. I unzip my pants so fast that sparks fly and she throws her head back, sliding books to the floor. Because she is a virgin, I proceed slowly, but she doesn't like it. She whispers gruff, filthy things in my ear, urging me to give it to her hard. Thinking of Sylvia Plath, I start to pull away, but she grabs my ass and jams my cock deep inside her.

I exploded at once, groaning so loudly that Chuck barked. Louise shoved me off, angry—not that I had come too quickly (which she considers a compliment) but that I had not pulled out beforehand. She actually thinks she's still fertile. It would be touching were it not so desperately delusional, and if she did not demand that I play along with her self-delusion. I cannot imagine being so vain that I would need my spouse to forsake her own sense of truth just so that I might feel young and viable. Tonight, for the first time, I could not do it.

"Jesus Christ, you're almost forty-six," I said. "You have as much chance of getting pregnant as Chuck does. And he's male! And fixed!"

She rolled to the wall with a strangled growl. This was my punishment for making her feel ridiculous. Well, fuck her. I threw back the covers. As I stepped into the hallway, I heard a deep sob. How many times have I found myself at this precise point of choice? Walk away and be wracked with guilt for days on end, or turn around, give comfort, and feel like an uxorious stooge. I returned to the bed, sat, and rubbed Louise's skinny neck. I told her that I was sorry, that of course she was still fertile. I was just feeling bitter because I had turned fifty. Her sobs turned to sniffles. She muttered a word I couldn't make out.

"What did you say?"

"Andropause."

"Come again?"

"Male menopause. It's what you're going through. I'm trying to be patient and understanding, but it's tough."

My body tingled. I felt a strange intuition that she knew I had lost my job but wasn't going to say anything about it until I did. Did she know about my escape plan too? Did she know about Nora? Was she reading my journal behind my back?

Louise rolled over, grabbed a tissue, and honked her red-tipped nose. Her smile was shy, pretty, and clueless. She knew nothing. She reached out her arms and pulled me onto her naked chest for wee, salty kisses. As I submitted, I was reminded of how excruciating it's going to be when I leave.

Sometimes I kid myself into believing that it won't be so bad, but deep down I know it will be the worst thing I've ever endured.

♦   ♦   ♦   ♦   ♦

I was huffing and puffing through a set of seventy-pound bench presses, when Archie's face floated into view. I expected him to mock me again, but instead he watched intently, betraying nothing. When I finished my set of twelve, he added eighty pounds to my rack.

"What are you doing?" I said, starting to get up. He stopped me with a hand to the chest.

"Try it."

"Why? I—"

"You can do it. Take a few deep breaths. Come on!"

I did as I was told.

"Okay, old man, give me ten."

"You're nuts."

"Make it twelve."

"Just wait until you're fifty and—"

"Fourteen! You can do it. Go!"

My face twisted, my back arched, and my legs flailed. I grunted out eight reps before I flopped into a gasping heap. I thought he would laugh at me, but instead he tapped my knee with his clipboard.

"Awesome."

"You said fourteen."

"Dude, I was joking. You just blew me away. How about tomorrow at noon for your free evaluation?"

"Smooth, but no thanks. I work Tuesdays."

"Okay, Wednesday. One o'clock."

I was just about to refuse again, when his huge brown eyes flashed and his lashes fluttered. Suddenly he was my little Archer, four years old and asking for a cookie. "A big, big one, Daddy. Please? I really love the big ones!" I was defenseless. I agreed to the appointment, and he grinned as he handed me his business card. I was sure that I'd feel resentful later, as though I'd been conned, but I'm actually getting excited. Maybe I don't have to surrender to old age after all.

◆ ◆ ◆ ◆ ◆

Whenever Big Peg hangs up after a stressful phone call, she looks over at me, deadpan, and says, "They jumped." It kills me every time. She is brilliantly funny, a virtue she displayed not a hint of when she trained me. It turns out that she spent six years as an unemployed actress before going back to school for her master's degree. She said that almost everyone in her program was an ex-artist of one sort or another. What is it about the study of psychology that attracts so many failures from the arts? Maybe it's because it's such an inexact science that it's almost impossible to blatantly fail. Bad pilots crash their planes. Bad surgeons kill their patients. Bad shrinks get book deals.

I could not have asked for a more colorful group of co-workers. Directly across from me sits Peg. Next to her is Trini Vizquel, a former Miss Venezuela, now in her late thirties, who takes all the Spanish calls. During her downtime, she talks about sex and how little action she gets from her elderly attorney husband. For the past seven years, she has been writing her doctoral dissertation on autoerotic asphyxiation. (Once I asked her to tell me the most surprising thing she'd learned about it. She said, "Remove your shoelaces and come here." Funny!) Last, near the kitchenette, sits Martha Lewey, a wiry, ex-police detective who lives in a log cabin with no power or indoor plumbing and thinks that we're all a bunch of pampered suburban pussies. In her spare time, she travels the globe, climbing mountains and winning triathlons. I made her laugh really hard once when I told her that I entered an over-fifty triathlon recently, where the events were long-distance biking, crapping your pants, and throwing up.

On my side of the room, I am by the door, then comes Tony Mazzocco, a beanpole former social worker with big sideburns, a major pot addiction, and a voice so deep and mellifluous it could put a rabid dog to sleep. He plays bass and sings for a rock band called Inbox Full. Last but not least, sitting near Henry's office door, is Kiki Davis, a high-strung ectomorph from Athens, Georgia, who, between calls, gives herself manicures and pedicures while chugging black coffee and popping black jelly beans. She refers to the callers as "customers," and her favorite joke is to cover the phone and whisper: "I'm in love!"

Adding to the general atmosphere of chaotic comedy is the fact that our telephone number is just one digit away from Lichtenstein Home Repair. Nothing like picking up the phone, braced for a life-and-death emergency, only to hear some batty yenta shriek, "You fix microwaves?"

I took only one serious call today, from a college freshman so addicted to a particular video game that he believes he lives inside it and that at any moment he is going to be attacked by a horde of zombies. He wanted to hang himself before they got there. He told me to tell his parents that he was sorry, but that he really had no choice—better hanged than devoured. Since it was obvious that he was a schizophrenic, I motioned to Peg, and with her help, I pulled off my first mobile crisis team referral. This is where a team that includes a shrink, a nurse, and a social worker races to the person's house. I waited with bated breath to hear the result, but we still hadn't heard when my shift ended, so I guess I'll find out next week.

♦ ♦ ♦ ♦ ♦

That summer in Paris, Louise and I spent two weeks at the Ritz, where our sleep was blissful, our mornings lazy, and our lovemaking perpetual. At night we dined at the best restaurants and drank at the hottest clubs; during the day, we mostly shopped. (Whenever I suggested we go to a museum, Louise explained that after an entire month in Aix-en-Provence, she was "arted out.") If I tried to pay for even so much as a taxi, Louise reacted as though I had spat in her face, and so I stopped trying. In short, I was a kept man, and to my surprise I liked it. I was often content, even at times happy, and with each passing day I felt more fondness for my benefactress. While I was not exactly falling in love with her, I had a crush on all that she provided.

Three weeks after our first kiss, my vacation was over. Time for me to fly home to face reality, which in this case meant job hunting in record humidity. Louise insisted on squiring me to Charles De Gaulle herself. In the limousine, I silently rehearsed my break-up speech—a tender but firm heave-ho to be delivered a few minutes before boarding the plane. She must have sensed that it was coming, because, just a few minutes into our ride, she announced that we were not, in fact, heading to the airport, but rather to Gare Saint-Lazare, where we would be hopping an express train for Cherbourg.

"What the hell's in Cherbourg?"

"*The Queen Elizabeth 2.* I booked us a first-class cabin. Don't even bother arguing, because I tore up your plane ticket."

I checked my money belt, and, sure enough, my non-refundable ticket, there just an hour ago, had vanished. To prove that I was still a man, I feigned righteous indignation for a minute or two, but inwardly I purred like a kitten. I had always wanted to travel by ocean liner, but never in my wildest dreams had I imagined that if I ever did it would be in anything but steerage.

Louise cozied up close. "I've always wanted to take the boat, but my mom said I had to wait and do it with the man I'm going to marry."

This would have been an ideal time to tell her that I was not that fellow. Instead I kissed her straight little nose and whispered something like "I'm glad you waited."

At sea, we were even more sybaritic than in Paris: We ate, drank, lounged in the sun, made love, watched movies, and, after a crash refresher course, even played a little duplicate bridge. I had imagined myself sitting on a deck chair as the sun bled into the vast Atlantic, finishing *Lord Jim* and waxing poetic in my journal, but I opened neither. I never even read a menu.

A few other things stand out in my memory. First, Louise kept bumping into people she knew, mostly friends of her parents. I, of course, knew no one. A gentle reminder that we came from different worlds. Second, one night in the casino, I dropped a hundred dollars at blackjack, a loss I could ill afford. The next morning three crisp hundred-dollar bills magically appeared in my wallet. Third, every single night after she fell asleep, I was forced to take a brisk walk around the deck in order to calm my anxiety. The source of my panic was obvious. I feared I lacked the strength of character to escape Louise and her golden cage.

From the West Side pier, we taxied straight to Louise's new high-rise apartment, which it turns out she had never seen before. Her parents had promised her that if she went to college close to home, they would buy her a co-op after her junior year. Well, the day had come, so that summer, while she was off studying Renoir, one of the family's household assistants had found and furnished for her a three-bedroom apartment at the edge of the Park. Evidently the assistant had done a heck of a job, because when Louise saw the place, she ran around screaming like a game-show contestant. She bounced on the couch, turned on the huge TV, even tested the kitchen faucet. I walked to a window, looked out at the soul-expanding view, and thought, Shit, no way I'm ever gonna leave.

Bill and Babs Carver were naturally eager to meet the dashing young novelist who had won the heart of their only child, so after just one night of dirtying her Egyptian-cotton sheets, we jumped into a hired car and headed north. The Carvers lived, and still live, ninety minutes north, in Birch Knoll, a turn-of-the-century manor house nestled in a private valley. It boasts a greenhouse and stables, and guest quarters into which my entire boyhood home could comfortably fit, yet it somehow manages to feel both graceful and austere. I remember when I walked into the gigantic pantry for the first time I saw two red riding jackets hanging from wooden pegs. I was astonished. I had thought fox hunting was illegal. I learned later that they were merely a design accent.

My parents were ugly, unwholesome creatures, ravaged by depression. Louise's parents were, by comparison, movie stars. I first glimpsed them walking across their vast back lawn. Were they really draped in muted tones of silk, suede, and cashmere, and swinging croquet mallets, or is this just a trick of memory? Next I remember Bill standing at the walnut bar, offering me a gin and tonic with an air of such debonair charm he might as well have been Fredric March. Babs was not at all the cold matriarch I had expected. She was energetic, funny, and lavishly affectionate. The first time she hugged me, I choked back a sob. It had been a long time since I had been touched by my own mother. As we sat and got acquainted, a butler continually materialized with tiny sterling bowls of nuts, chips, and candies. At one point, a plump female cook cleared her throat and said that she needed to get started on the evening's menu. Since I was the guest of honor, Babs insisted I make the final decision. Filet mignon, lobster, or both?

"Both," I replied nonchalantly.

After dinner, I had to use the bathroom. Requiring privacy, I walked right past the john that the servant had pointed out, and went off in search of something more discreet. Even the second floor was a bit too public for my tastes, so I climbed a narrow Victorian staircase, fitted with a funicular wheelchair for the infirm. The third floor, which had housed the household staff before separate quarters were built, was all but abandoned. The air was sharp with mothballs. I opened three doors at random, each revealing a big dusty room crowded with clothes racks, storage boxes, and old steamer trunks. Behind the fourth door, I found a big, shiny bathroom. I smiled when I saw yesterday's *Wall Street Journal* lying on the floor and the brown butt of one of Bill's Canadian cigarettes on the window sill. Dad liked privacy, too.

I opened the toilet and stepped back in horror. At the bottom of the bowl sat an enormous turd, bent like a comma. The water was rusty. No toilet paper floated above it. Why not?

I flushed as quickly as I could. The offense exploded into flaky shrapnel. For years whenever I thought of Bill Carver and his fortune, I saw that shocking leave-behind and pondered the mysterious absence of paper. Did it reveal something about the rich that I would never be able to fathom? Or was it an omen that I did not know how to read?

♦ ♦ ♦ ♦ ♦

During a cigarette break today, Big Peg told me that she had read an article this morning that said suicide, along with chocolate, sleeping pills, and booze, is doing a boom business. It isn't just a result of the recession and the long years of war—it's also that so many mentally ill people are being denied treatment by underfunded public programs. She was not surprised by this at all, as our call load has been up 25% this year, and just last week she attended the funeral of a high school pal, a financial consultant and father of three, who, since losing his job had been a househusband. On the way to Price Chopper one afternoon to pick up diapers and orange juice, he parked his BMW in the middle of the Rip Van Winkle Bridge and jumped. On the way down his arm got caught on an iron support and was practically pulled off before he disengaged and landed on the cement base.

I came back with a related tale plucked from the week's headlines. The other day in China, a young man clung to a bridge, contemplating suicide and holding up traffic. An elderly man somehow toddled through the police cordon, walked over to the suicidal man, shook his hand, and pushed him off the bridge. The old man said he'd lost patience with the guy's selfishness. Peg and I chuckled over that one. No one is more selfish than our callers.

✦ ✦ ✦ ✦ ✦

A novel: everything that flashes through the hero's mind between the moment he jumps and the moment he lands.

✦ ✦ ✦ ✦ ✦

Robert Louis Stevenson: "If you are going to make a book end badly, it must end badly from the beginning."

✦ ✦ ✦ ✦ ✦

Archie conducted my free fitness evaluation today. His verdict was hardly earth-shattering: I am a stiff weakling. He said that my early engagement in competitive sports has put me in good stead to regain my muscle bulk and tone, but that my core needs serious work. I was too embarrassed to ask for a definition. He proposed a program of stretching and light weightlifting. Just an hour a week to start. I figure, what the hell. At worst, I will firm up my pectorals before they turn into bona fide bosoms; at best, I will prolong my life. So what if it's expensive? I'm worth it.

✦ ✦ ✦ ✦ ✦

Archie mentioned in passing that he was six years old when his father died. I asked him his dad's name. If he had said Malcolm, I would have fainted. His dad's name was Trent. Is Archie my Stephen Dedalus?

✦ ✦ ✦ ✦ ✦

Interesting call at work: A born-again Christian, recently abandoned by her husband, spent the night at her best girlfriend's house. They shared the bed because her pal's husband, a salesman, was out of town and wouldn't be back until the following afternoon. Well, it turns out the husband arrived home early to surprise his wife. The surprise was on him, of course, when he found two naked women in his bed. When neither woke up at his entrance, he crawled under the covers and went down on the caller for fifteen minutes.

Anguished, she was now contemplating suicide. "My hands are shaking!" she screamed at me. "My hands are shaking!" I asked her a few obvious questions and learned that, although she had woken up at the first touch of the husband's tongue, she had not actually pushed his head away until after she had orgasmed, and that her hands did not start shaking until three days later, not because she was ashamed of what she had done but because the husband had threatened, merely in jest, to tell his wife.

I told her that she secretly resented and envied her friend's marital stability and that her betrayal of her friend was, in some perverse way, revenge on her own husband for betraying her. She fought me every step of the way. Finally, I lost my temper and told her that she was not suicidal at all, just hypocritical and horny. I told her not to tie up our phone lines with her self-indulgent nonsense, and I hung up in her face. After a few deep breaths, I looked around. Everyone was either on a call or on a break. No one had overheard me. Phew.

◆ ◆ ◆ ◆ ◆

A person endowed with a vivid imagination can transport himself out of any situation. For instance, if I were in solitary confinement at Sing Sing, I could keep myself entertained simply by daydreaming. I have had much practice at this. Many nights have I lain next to my slumbering wife and let my mind carry me back to women I made love to before I got married, or should have. At other times I invent a woman to make love to. Sometimes a fantasy will be so vivid that when I wake up I believe that she is real. As far as the human brain is concerned, fantasy and memory are identical. Studies have proved it.

On a grander ontological level, this gift is also useful in terms of aging. As my body changes, softening and wrinkling, I simply replace the truth with my own fantasy of how I look. As my death grows closer, this fantasy will bring me much comfort. A dismal fate: slavery to the facts. Give me the imagination any day.

♦　♦　♦　♦　♦

At dinner tonight, Karen tapped her water glass with her butter knife and announced that she had an announcement.

"I got a job. At the Sleepy Valley Animal Hospital."

Louise and I cheered and clapped. Rosa cried out in Spanish, something along the lines of Ooo-la-la. I raised my wine-glass and gushed about how proud I was that my girl had found a summer job despite the recession.

"It was easy," Karen shrugged. "I told them they didn't have to pay me."

♦　♦　♦　♦　♦

Nora Woodling and I spent almost all of today's lunch discussing my new apartment. I explained that I wanted to buy instead of rent and that I required a minimum of three bedrooms so that she would have her own home office. She laughed as though I were joking. As for location, I told her that I had settled on Bedford Heights, so that I would be within striking distance of my girls when they are home visiting their mother.

"Is that okay with you?" I asked.

"What do you mean?"

"Living so far north?"

"Oh, please, Mr. Poe—"

"Stop being coy. You know as well as I do that this place is for both of us."

Hopeful tears sprang into her timid eyes. I grabbed her hands across the table, and, gazing at her, thought: No one has ever cared for this woman as I do. She has never found a home in the heart of another. She believed herself destined to loneliness. We are going to make love and art together, and enjoy more happiness than any two people deserve.

I let go of her hands and fell back into the booth. I think she was astonished that I did not try to kiss her. Instead, I picked up right where I had left off. I told her I wanted a terrace with a river view. A doorman might be nice, too. She said not to worry about anything, that she would handle it all and find me exactly what I wanted. She laughed at my bewildered expression and explained that she had worked for a real estate attorney for almost a year, and that even though she still hoped my marriage could be saved, if I was hell-bent on leaving, she wanted to make sure that I found a suitable home.

♦ ♦ ♦ ♦ ♦

All of these years I have regretted never having written a novel, but what if it's only because I am, in fact, a born poet?

◆   ◆   ◆   ◆   ◆

Intimate celebration of Louise's forty-sixth birthday. I gave her the skin rejuvenation contraption she wanted and a card full of fresh thoughts and sentiments. Then we sat down to a candlelight dinner, and a Tragedy of Inconsequence in one scene:

"You seem distant," she said.

"I do?"

"More than usual."

"Huh."

"How come?"

"Beats me."

"How's work?"

"The same. Always the same."

"Really?"

"We're running a story on Wall Street suicides. Happens more often than you think. Last month, a hedge fund manager cut his own throat right before his sentencing hearing."

"Sad."

"I guess."

"You guess?"

"Some of them are probably better off."

"What a terrible thing to say."

"Yeah, but is it true? Isn't that the more important question? The most important question? Whether it's true?"

"People who kill themselves are mentally ill. They need help. Life's always preferable to death."

"Oh, really? What the hell do you know about human suffering?"

Louise glared at me, set her jaw, and pushed back her plate, knocking over a crystal candlestick. Red wax splashed the Irish linen. As she stormed out, I righted the candle and called for Rosa. Normally I would have followed Louise upstairs, but I ducked down here instead. I hate when she doesn't stand her ground and makes me chase her. Why was her reaction so violent, anyway? Was it that my question struck at the quick of her rich girl insecurities, or was it the implication that she had not suffered deeply enough in the wake of Archer's death?

♦ ♦ ♦ ♦ ♦

I had a wet dream last night. First time in more than thirty years. It must be because I have not masturbated in weeks due to my burning prostate. I woke up crusty and happy, and why not? I had just made love to Nora. So vivid. I took her virginity on a Mediterranean beach. I was gentle and patient. She did not hemorrhage. And guess what? My prostate no longer hurts. Must have been a deep orgasm that broke up some sort of blockage. Which brings to mind a quotation I once read. A contemporary female novelist whose name I forget said that adolescence resembles middle age in that in both cases a person is barely under control. How true. There are days when I feel that I am barely hanging on. And what is a wet dream but a loss of self-control at the most elemental, gonadic level? Surely there are major differences between a boy of sixteen and a man of fifty, but right now they elude me—except for the most obvious one: The former is growing hair where he wants it, and the latter is growing hair where he doesn't. How can anyone believe in intelligent design when there is such a thing as late-onset ear and nose hair? On the other hand, I doubt the Darwinists can account for it either. No selective advantage in being repulsive. I'm rambling. Finish my drink and up to bed. Chuck just yawned hugely (as though he had read this entry). Oh no, just had a depressing thought. Who will get custody of Chuck after the split? I bought him, but Louise walks and feeds him. The girls will never forgive me if I spirit him away, but I'm not sure I can bear to part with him. He's the only one in this family that understands me.

Speak of the devil, Louise is calling from upstairs. Something tripped the backyard security lights, and she fears an intruder. There isn't one, but Chuck and I will grab a flashlight and investigate anyway. Because that's what a man does.

◆   ◆   ◆   ◆   ◆

An old woman called today, requesting information on assisted suicide for her husband, who has "the Lou Gehrig." I told her that we are in the business of saving lives, not ending them. She offered a simple-minded defense of euthanasia that I could barely make out because across the aisle Trini Vizquel was coughing up her lungs.

After my call had ended, I asked Trini, "Been checked for TB lately?"

She stared at me long and hard—not angry just deciding—then she wheeled her chair over and said that her last caller was a convicted child molester, and that after he'd told her this, she had started to cough uncontrollably.

"Why do you think that was?"

"Probably because when I was a little girl, my abuelito used to make me suck his dick."

"Oh no! Are you serious?"

"'Abuelito' means grandfather."

"I know what it means! Why are you telling me this?"

"Too much information!" Peg boomed with a grin.

All the other workers laughed. Turns out, Trini's lack of boundaries is common knowledge. Nothing would have been easier than for her to have answered me with a half-truth or an evasion, and yet she felt entitled to befoul my imagination with the image of her wrinkly old grampa sitting in a wicker chair with no pants on, munching a coca leaf beneath a slow-moving fan while she ministered to his cock. But it's useless to single out Trini. It's the whole culture! Discretion is dead. Strangers swap their darkest secrets like cookie recipes. Foreigners arrive on our shores and within months they can't shut up either. It's a national plague. I should have been born in Finland, where people keep their dirty laundry in hampers and rarely utter a word.

♦ ♦ ♦ ♦ ♦

A girl just called, crying so hard that I thought her wrists were already open. Two weeks ago, she was in the shower when she heard gunshots, ran downstairs, and found her kid brother, just eighteen, shot twice in the chest. He died before the ambulance arrived. Her drug-dealing ex-boyfriend had vowed to make her pay for breaking up with him while he was in jail, so she knew who the killer was. She also knew that if she told the police, he would kill her next. She hasn't told anyone, and now she can't sleep, eat, or concentrate at work. (Luckily, she inputs data for the Department of Motor Vehicles, so no one has noticed.) She wants to die, she said, because she can't forgive God for letting her ex get away with murder.

I was tempted to tell her that it was not God who let him

get away with it, but she. Instead I told her that I knew exactly how she felt because a decade ago I had lost a son whose big chocolate eyes and thick eyelashes haunt me still. She asked me how it happened and I told her the whole story. Soon she wasn't crying anymore. It was like one of those explosions they use to blow out oil-well fires. My greater tragedy obliterated hers. I found her a therapist and invited her to call back anytime.

After I hung up, I felt sick to my stomach. I remembered how, for months after Archer died, I heard his piping voice everywhere I went. Daddy, will you blow bubbles with me? Daddy, can I stand on your shoulders? Daddy, time to read a book! The pain never goes away. Henry Glover let me go home an hour early.

◆ ◆ ◆ ◆ ◆

Dinner last night with the McNamaras, Pisanis, and Shapiros. All people talked to me about were their investments. Now I know how doctors feel when all people talk about are their sciatica and hemorrhoids. I wanted to scream, "Money isn't life! It's death!" I gorged instead. The risotto was excellent. So was the tiramisu. I did not embarrass Louise once.

◆ ◆ ◆ ◆ ◆

When I arrived at the shop this morning as instructed, Nora, busy with a customer, discreetly handed me an envelope. Inside was a typed list of five co-op apartments within walking distance of Fort Tryon Park. At the bottom she wrote in her pretty feminine hand that the reason none of them has a river view is that it adds half a million dollars to the cost, which struck her as a "daft extravagance." I love that Nora is looking out for my financial best interests and uses words like "daft."

I am sitting on the subway now, rattling uptown to see the apartments. With every jostle, an ancient Chinese or Korean man presses the side of his leg against mine. I don't know if it's intentional, but I am perfectly happy never to find out. It will be wonderful to see Washington Heights again. I expect many warm memories to return of my three weeks with Gianna. What was her last name? Starts with a W. It will come to me. I was just out of Yale, and she was studying to be a cop. The park was our second home. We strolled its promenades, gazing out at the unparalleled views of the mighty river, and because we both had roommates, a few times we fucked in the bushes. Once we even did it inside the Cloisters itself. I wonder if Nora knows the Cloisters. I would think medieval French monasteries are right up her virgin alley. I bet it will take at least a few years of conventional sex before she would even consider doing it outside, let alone in a chapel. But you never know. Once the floodgates of a woman's sexuality are open, anything's possible.

The broker for all of Nora's listings is Jack Trippet. I asked if he could show me all five this morning, and he said, "When can you get here?" If I find a place that I love, I'll put in an immediate offer. I'm ready. No need for anxious second guessing. My marriage ends roughly three months from today.

Because Louise is an avid cuddler, for the past twenty-five years we have slept in a queen-size bed that I cannot bear. At last I can buy the king-size bed for which I've yearned. It's the first piece of furniture I'll move into the new place. Maybe as the day nears and Nora sees that my feelings for her are sincere, she will make love to me in the bed that day it arrives, before I have even moved in the rest of my stuff. Stop it, Mal.

Daydreams are dangerous. You will get ahead of yourself.

Wojcik. Gianna Wojcik. Yes, that was her name. In high school they called her the Italian Pole because of her mixed heritage and because she was so tall and skinny. But what a face she had. Her height allowed us to do it standing up against trees. She hated me after I dumped her. I don't blame her. It was abrupt. But I knew that we were incompatible. She was functionally illiterate. I wonder where she is today.

◆　◆　◆　◆　◆

I love the subway. I look forward to using it more often. It is an invaluable resource for an urban writer. I would love to publish short stories for *The New Yorker* inspired by different female subway riders, and then compile them into a sort of subterranean *Winesburg, Ohio*. For example, I overheard the following lines just this morning. From an acne-faced blonde with a huge ass: "I gave myself one when I was in high school by jumping off a house." Shrill Brooklyn mom: "I'm telling you, he has a hole in his heart from all the drugs." Bronx loudmouth with flagrant nose job: "So I says, 'It ain't rocket scientry, asshole.'" Big mama with scary, sparkly fingernails: "He ain't nut'in' but a black male sterile-type."

◆　◆　◆　◆　◆

I had a good feeling about the building the moment I saw the cool, dark, immaculate lobby adorned with a white-haired Irish doorman reading the *Irish Times* and a WPA mural depicting the swindling of the Injuns. A shiny, antique elevator with brass controls carried me to the fifth floor, where Jack Trippet was already waiting. The apartment is gorgeous:

high, beamed ceilings, parquet floors, original fixtures, and big, sunny windows. I can't imagine a better place to begin the third act of my life. I told Jack I didn't even need to see the other apartments on the list. He insisted I at least take a peek. I told him to learn to take yes for an answer. He gave me the building's rule book, which details my ownership rights and the building's tax structure. Once Nora has okayed the place, I will give them their asking price. Why play hard to get?

◆　◆　◆　◆　◆

Just Googled Gianna Wojcik. Found a testimonial from her brother, written six years ago. She was shot and killed by her boyfriend. A fellow cop. I wonder if her memory will haunt me as I stroll the park.

◆　◆　◆　◆　◆

As I walked into the health club today for my first training session, it occurred to me that, having spent the past quarter century steering the family ship on a sea of estrogen, I am fairly expert on the subject of young women, and yet I know very little about young men. (Unless you count the bumptious frat boys with their yellow ties and chunky thighs crammed into wrinkled khakis, who over the years arrived at the magazine in search of employment. I don't count them. Anyone who, fresh out of college, wants to work at *Investors Monthly* is a soulless shit.) This meant that my time training with Archie would be my first prolonged exposure to red-blooded American male youth. I vowed to take literary advantage of it.

As we worked, I grilled Archie without tact or shame. This is what I learned: Archibald John Anglesey, nineteen, hails

from rural Vermont, where his father, Trent, was an organic
vegetable farmer and his mother, Tammy, a hired hand. They
married when Trent was forty-three and Tammy twenty-one.
Trent died at forty-seven while shoveling snow.

"From an aneurysm," Archie explained. "Or was it an
embolism?"

This joke revealed Archie's absolute detachment from the
man he hardly knew. His mother remarried, to a kind-hearted
insurance salesman named Wade Lamb, a taciturn fellow
Archie loves but feels he doesn't really know. Growing up,
Archie was a mediocre student, but a gifted martial artist and
tumbler. He dreamt of a career as a stuntman until his best
friend was paralyzed from the chest down in a snowboarding
accident. When a cousin called and said that the Manhattan
health club where he worked needed a kickboxing instructor,
Archie hopped the next bus. He has been a New Yorker for
only eight months, sleeping on his cousin's couch in Astoria,
but he already knows he will never leave. Based on what he
told me, I would say that his single greatest obstacle to success
is his daily marijuana habit, which renders him too easygoing
for his own good. For example:

"So what do you want to do?"

"You mean when I grow up?"

"If you grow up."

"I dunno. This? Or maybe something else?"

"So you've narrowed it down."

"Pretty much. Maybe I'll own a martial arts academy?"

"What's with the question marks at the end of your
statements? Are you asking me or telling me?"

"Both?"

During a particularly grueling series of stretches, Archie's
counting tapered off to a whisper. I rolled off the big rubber

ball and plopped to the floor. He did not even notice. I looked over and there, not fifteen feet away, was Veronica Veronique, the demented porno actress, lying flat on her back, scissoring her legs. She wore short silky red trunks. Each time her legs began to swing closed, her entire pubic mound, clad in white silk, was visible for a full half second. Archie's eyes feasted on its hairless, bipartite beauty. So did mine. We breathed in unison. A moment of exquisite bonding.

"She's not much older than you are," I mumbled. "Go say hi."

"My cousin talked to her last week. She's into old dudes with money."

"Like me."

"That's what I'm sayin', dude. Go for it."

"No thanks. I'm in love. With a virgin."

"I thought you were married with kids."

"Not for long, dude."

Suddenly her legs fell to the mat. She lay there, chest heaving, her limbs wide apart as though she were making a snow angel. Her peasant face was glazed with sweat. Her nipples were erect and as crinkly as chewed gum. Just as I was about to note to Archie how bizarre it was that she was a complete stranger, and yet, due to the miracle of the Internet, I had already seen her ravaged stem to stern, she popped up like a toy and smiled right at me. I felt ridiculous, ten pounds overweight and leaning against a huge blue ball with my hair askew. And yet her unblinking smile brimmed with the sort of crazy, unashamed lust that I had not inspired since Starla Ferris. Or whatever her name was.

◆ ◆ ◆ ◆ ◆

This morning, when Louise asked me why I was walking like Frankenstein (she meant his monster), I told her about my training session with Archie. From her violent reaction, you would have thought I'd said I had taken up sword-swallowing or survived a fall from a dirigible.

"A trainer? Why?"

"So you'll find me sexy again."

She scrunched her face, uncertain as to whether I was joking. Before she could decide, I ducked into the john. It's funny how spouses know each other so well that the tiniest deviation from routine can send them into a panic. I don't blame her for being suspicious, I guess. Since I hit around forty, I have shown almost no interest in exercise. I remember when she gave me the club membership, I smirked and said, "Any excuse to spend money, huh?" The girls leapt down my throat for being rude and ungrateful, and I suppose they were right, but I was sure I would never use it.

By the time I emerged from the bathroom, Louise's panic had been supplanted by pride. She gave me a big hug, squeezed my ass, and said, "In training for the empty nest?"

I laughed. "What do you mean?"

"All the sex we're gonna have. We can do it whenever we want."

For one of the few times in my life, I was speechless. Rather than struggle for the right words to deceive or amuse her, I lowered her onto the bed and gave her a sound fucking. The whole time, I imagined that she was Veronica Veronique and there were cameras in every corner of the room.

◆　◆　◆　◆　◆

Henry Glover just called me into his office to tell me that

based on a review of the phone logs, I take roughly the same number of calls as my co-workers, but spend far less time on the phone. He infers from this that either my callers are swiftly satisfied or they can't wait to hang up and kill themselves.

"Lucky for you," he said with a rascally smile, "we'll never know which one it is. See, when we prevent a suicide, we sometimes get a thank-you call, but when we cause one, not a peep. I don't know why." He burst out laughing and sat forward. "Another thing. Your case reports are way too short."

"I was told the length was up to us."

"It is, but come on, man." He picked up a sheet of paper and recited what I had written. "'Male nurse. Hates his dreadful mother. Called to whine about it. Sounds gay.'"

"Yeah, so?"

He read the next one: "'Old man dying alone at home. No family. I wonder why he's depressed.'"

"So is sarcasm also—"

And another: "'Russian immigrant, blathering gibberish. Next!'" Henry lay down the sheets and squeaked back in his chair. "Those aren't case reports. They're tweets!"

He laughed and laughed.

What a happy-go-lucky fellow he is. If I were in his position, I would have fired me on the spot. It's as though he couldn't care less about his job. As a rule, black Republicans are an enigma to me, anyway, but this guy is particularly puzzling.

◆　◆　◆　◆　◆

Chuck is sluggish. He's almost eleven and his father died at ten. I pray he's not beginning to fail. I have made up my mind to take him with me. I dream of walking him along the river as the first dead leaves flutter down in the chill autumn dusk.

◆ ◆ ◆ ◆ ◆

Despite whatever comfort I derive from my writing and my budding romance with Nora, moments of profound loneliness lie ahead for me. I know this, and yet I am unafraid. G. K. Chesterton said: "A thing created is loved before it exists." Although it is not yet born, I already love my new life of emotional, sexual, and creative freedom.

◆ ◆ ◆ ◆ ◆

I just read that the Himalayan glaciers, which supply water to a billion people, will be gone in less than twenty years. Is the whole thing finished? Is mankind on its last legs? When I try to share my fears with Louise, she practically plugs her ears and sings nursery rhymes to herself. She says that as a mother it is too painful to hear these things. Well, as a husband it is painful to be starved for adult conversation. Louise and many others who come from old money, believe that if you do not discuss something it does not exist. They are members of the Ostrich School. (An excellent title for a novel.) I believe that discussing terrifying things is the first step in conquering them. A sad irony that the trait I prize most in others—candor—is absent in my wife.

◆ ◆ ◆ ◆ ◆

Nora finally saw the co-op. Walking from room to room, she praised certain details that I had entirely missed—crown moldings, pockets doors, original doorknobs. She has a keen eye and superb taste. I encouraged her to think of the place as her own, but she refused, reminding me that I am still a married man. When I asked her to at least tell me which room, if she lived here, she would use as her study, she laughed as though I were a lunatic. And yet I know she shares the fantasy, because when she saw the big kitchen, she blushed like a new bride and her eyes got wet.

"You like to cook?" I whispered in her ear, my hands settling on her fragile shoulders.

Her silence said yes, then she shrank away and opened the broom closet.

"Good," I said, "because I'd rather have a wife that cooks than one who speaks Greek."

She shot me a dirty look.

"Hey, don't blame me," I laughed. "Dr. Johnson said it!"

"He said lots of crap," she replied.

Later, on the sidewalk, Jack Trippet told us what to expect. Once my offer is accepted, my attorney will review the building's finances. If everything is up to snuff, I then submit a deposit of 10 percent, an application, a financial statement, three years of federal tax returns, letters of reference, and a letter from the mortgage company saying that my mortgage has already been approved. If all of it's in order, I'll be asked to meet the co-op board. I'll face them alone—no brokers, no attorneys—and I must answer any personal questions they throw my way. Do I smoke? Do I play the trumpet? Do I have a pet python? Any there any teenagers in my life? He told me to stress the fact that I am a novelist and that all I want is a quiet place to work. This will be easy for me, as it happens to be the truth.

After Jack jumped into a cab, I offered Nora a lift home. She protested that surely I had better things to do on a Saturday afternoon than drive to Brooklyn, but I assured her that I did not. I had told Louise that I was visiting Sid Davis in the hospital after his emergency angioplasty. Impressed with my kindness, Louise had ordered Carmen to whip up a batch of chocolate chip cookies. Just what the doctor orders for clogged arteries.

The drive was pure happiness. Nora opened up about her childhood as she never has before. She told me that her only refuge from the drunken tirades of her disabled father and the sadism of her siblings was her piano. She spent hours after school in the storage room behind the gym, practicing on a forgotten upright, imagining that its chipped black and white keys represented all the clashing forces of evil and good in her home and that only she had the magical power to draw them into harmony. (A common sort of fantasy, I suspect, among the children of alcoholics.) After her freshman year at St. Olaf, she quit piano to become a poetess. Furious, her father cut her off financially, and she was forced to drop out of school.

I said: "I know a lot of people who gave up their instruments as kids, then started up again as adults and really loved it. Any desire?"

"I can't afford a piano."

"I'll get you one."

"Don't say that."

"I will. And if the co-op board objects, I'll buy you an electronic one with headphones."

"Malcolm, it's very sweet of you to say these things, but you really shouldn't. It confuses me. We hardly know each other. Really." I started to argue with her, but she cut me off. "It's true. I worked for you years ago, and now we've had a few lunches and—"

"I'm crazy about you."

"You're not," she protested. "Stop it!"

"I love your Celtic fire."

"Aha, you see!" she cried, fighting a smile. "I'm not Celtic. I'm English, Norwegian, and French."

"Whatever. I love your passion. And your brains. And your high ideals. And your—"

To silence me, she laid a hand on mine atop the gear shift. With the other hand, she wiped a tear from her eye. It's a good thing I was driving, otherwise I might have kissed her. I opened the windows and turned on the radio. The hot wind whipped her hair. She sniffled, turned from my classical station to a pop station, and started to sing along, doing jerky little dance moves with her arms and shoulders. I had not been so happy in years. When she plugged her nose and pretended to shimmy under the waves, I laughed so hard I almost crashed.

What I have been unable to shake from our day together is her smelly, dismal brownstone. Her racist landlady clearly has not invested a penny since her husband's death a decade ago. Half the front banister is missing. Most of the green shutters are crooked or missing, and the windows are opaque with grime. Nora said that a morbidly obese postman lives on the top floor, and a surly Dominican meter maid dwells in the basement. Nora and the widow share the second floor, including the bathroom. Miserable existence. I must rescue her.

◆　◆　◆　◆　◆

Spent an hour with Alan Hapgood this morning discussing my purchase of the co-op. As he has known Louise and me socially for almost twelve years, he was uncomfortable with the idea of representing me behind her back, but in the end he agreed. He said he did it because he doesn't want to lose me as a friend. I think the real reason is that he knows if our break up turns ugly, some lucky divorce lawyer is going to make a bundle, and it might as well be someone from his firm.

◆　◆　◆　◆　◆

Everyone is saving a life right now except me, who scribbles in this journal, and Kiki Davis, who pops black jelly beans into her gob while reading a trashy novel. She turns the pages delicately because her red nails are still wet. We all know better than to ask Kiki to share her treats, so we content ourselves with the bowl of lemon sours that magically replenishes itself each night. The level-headed say it is not the handiwork of a magical kitchen elf but the generosity of a colleague on the graveyard shift. Above the bowl of lemon candy, takeout menus hang willy-nilly on a bulletin board, along with government pamphlets on self-slaughter. Inside the refrigerator sit containers of food with notes taped to them like "Don't you dare!" and "Eat me upon pain of death!" I am tempted to turn on the TV and learn more about the state of the world, but why bother when any second my phone might ring. Anyway, the TV is only here to keep the graveyard workers awake during the desolate hours between 5 and 9 a.m. when the genuinely miserable have already killed themselves and the fakers have finally hit the hay.

◆　◆　◆　◆　◆

Something remarkable occurred at the end of today's shift. I was sharing a cigarette with Big Peg when I suddenly found myself telling her the whole truth about my marriage. She listened so patiently and empathically that I realized with a jolt how blind I've been: I am in desperate need of therapy. My marriage has been hell for years, but ending it will be a worse hell unless I achieve as much clarity as possible. Why not make Big Peg my shrink? She's a trained professional, and we enjoy a warm and wonderful rapport. I will not tell her that she is my shrink, of course. She will just think that we are good friends, and I do most of the talking.

◆ ◆ ◆ ◆ ◆

My father never cared to know me. My mother knows me only as the unplanned child whose difficult delivery ruined her body and whose watchful eyes recorded every nuance of her moral decline. My daughters know me only as the easygoing dad who never interferes when their mom spoils them. Louise knows me only as her loyal, grumpy spouse. My in-laws are impressed by my steadfast dedication to my humdrum job. Before I die, I would like to stand naked, just once, before another human being—no secrets, roles, lies, or masks—and be seen.

I have chosen you, Nora Ann Woodling, to be this witness. Tomorrow at lunch I will hand you an exquisitely wrapped gift and ask that you not open it until the following day, your thirty-ninth birthday. Despite your excitement, I know that you will comply with my request. My hope is that you will open the gift in the morning when you're still in bed and that you'll become so helplessly engrossed in the first book that you'll be unable to put it down and will cancel all your Saturday plans. (This despite your ethical objection to reading the intimate journal of a married man.) After you're finished, I'm hoping that you'll move directly to the second book and that by the time you read these words, you'll understand that nothing else I could have given you would have expressed even half as much love and trust. Oh, my dearest girl, are you still snug in your bed? Has the sun climbed high into the sky?

In ten short weeks, I will be settled into my new home, available to you any hour of the day or night. Although I'm a half century old, I know little of romantic love, save for what you have taught me. I will be just as frightened as you are when we merge for the first time. In the words of the great Leo Tolstoy: "I already love you in your beauty, but I am only beginning to love in you that which is eternal and ever precious—your heart, your soul."

Yes, your heart and soul.

And now the great Dostoevsky: "In the past it was only her infernal curves that tortured me, but now I've taken all her soul into my soul, and through her I've become a man myself."

I know what you are thinking: "Surely, Mr. Poe, you've had too many Scotches."

All right, maybe a few too many, but they've only lubricated my veracity! Call me when you are finished reading! Good night! Good night! Good night!

BOOK THREE

Although a journal cannot be classified as a work of art, more of my flesh and blood lives in the two notebooks that I gave Nora than in anything I have ever created (with the exception of my daughters, of course), and if there is one thing conspicuously missing from today's literature it is flesh and blood. I want so badly to know whether Nora feels the pulse of truth beating inside each and every word that I can scarcely concentrate enough to begin this third volume. My hope is that the journals will confirm for her what she claims to believe already: first, that I am a good man who has behaved honorably in an impossible situation; second, that I am destined for great things. Anything less than this and I'm afraid I might collapse inward, revert to my smallest self, lose the courage to begin again. A sad testament to my resolve, I know, but, for better or worse, Nora has become my muse. If my intimate confessions do not confirm for her my worth, both as a man and an artist, what chance do I have among those who are indifferent to begin with? It's a good thing Nora refused me her home phone number, or I would be pestering her already, which would be a disaster for my self-respect.

◆   ◆   ◆   ◆   ◆

Wedding bells: After my first weekend at Birch Knoll, my romance with Louise (to rustle a cliché from the stables) broke into a gallop. No time for sober judgment now or even clear perception, because overnight we were swept into a blur of garden parties, soirées, luncheons, cookouts, and teas. Wearing fancy new duds that Louise had bought me in Paris, I was transformed from a toilet-burnishing drudge into a society darling. Everyone wanted to meet the tall, dashing novelist who had captured the heart of Louise Jane Carver, heiress to one of the largest cash trusts on the Eastern Seaboard. I disliked most of the people I met, but I would be lying if I did not confess to a perverse fascination with their baseless arrogance and effortless, shallow charm.

Just one dark cloud: I possessed an actual soul, and, once born a soul can never be silenced. Every night in bed when I closed my eyes, it whispered that no matter how dazzled I was by Vanity Fair, I was neither a merchant nor a customer and did not belong there. To rationalize staying, I told myself that I was a spy behind enemy lines whose sole mission it was to keep my eyes open and wits clear until the hour of my escape. My findings would be delivered in the form of a brilliant satirical novel.

The Carvers had other ideas. What Lou-Lou wanted Lou-Lou got, and they had no intention of letting me escape her clutches. While I had enough moral fiber to resist their bribes, I found it harder to resist their admiration. Not only did they not hold it against me that my drunken father had hanged himself and that the only difference between my mother and a whore was that a whore had better business sense, but they hailed me for overcoming their influences. They boasted to their friends that I had come from absolutely nothing, had attended both Groton and Yale on full scholarship, and was now on my way to a great literary career. At first, I was bewildered by their high opinion of me, but in time I came to understand it.

Fitzgerald once wrote, "The rich are different from you and me." To which Hemingway replied something along the lines of "Yes, they have more money." Scott, as usual, was closer to the truth than Papa, although I'm not sure he was objective or sober enough to know exactly what those differences were. Having lived half of my life in close proximity to fabulous wealth, I can state with serene confidence that people born to old money *are* different from us: They are far more susceptible to boredom, nostalgia, and self-doubt. Naturally they admire anyone who makes his own way in the world, because they suspect that if they had been forced to fend for themselves, they would have ended up gibbering and naked, eating fish bones out of dumpsters.

Equally bewildering to me was that the Carvers did not seem to mind in the least that I was jobless and flat broke. If Louise believed in me, that was good enough for them. Also, it was a foregone conclusion that when my debut novel was finished it would be published, and from there it would be a hop, skip, and a jump to the Pulitzer Prize. I nurtured this fantasy by never letting on that my debut novel did not actually exist. One Sunday at Birch Knoll, I excused myself to "get some work done," but instead I took a delicious nap. When I shuffled downstairs two hours later, digging a knuckle into my eye, Babs said, "Ollie was chasing a rabbit. I hope his barking didn't bother you. I know a lot of writers need complete silence." I answered, stone-faced: "I sure do. I'm like Carlyle, hypersensitive to sound. But don't worry about Ollie. I brought along earplugs. I never go anywhere without them." My big smile told her that I had made brilliant progress on my book that afternoon.

While Birch Knoll had impressed me, when, the very next week, I beheld the Carvers' Nantucket estate, Squam Hut, I was struck dumb. As grand and gorgeous as any other property on the island, it boasts a tennis court, a swimming pool, terraced gardens, and a half-mile stretch of private beach. As at Birch Knoll, I was not permitted to share a bedroom with Louise, but I minded it even less here, because the guest quarters were a three-bedroom cabin with an ocean view, a fire pit, a hot tub, and a full bar.

A few days later, on the Thursday before Labor Day, Louise and her mother hopped a plane to Boston for a day of shopping. I remember thinking how odd this was, given that Louise had just shopped herself silly in Paris and how desperately she hated to be away from me even for a second. Bill was on the links that day, so I was left alone. An early autumn chill was in the air, and fog billowed in from the sea. I sat alone on my front porch, sipping a hot toddy and reading *The Mill on the Floss*. Probably because the book centers on the conflict between passion and duty, I found myself lowering the book again and again to reflect on my dilemma. I was not in love with Louise but I liked her very much, and I loved that she loved me. I thought of Eva, whom I had adored almost on sight, and Starla, the thought of whose nakedness still made me demented with desire. Was it a serious problem that nothing I felt for Louise came close to matching either of these intensities?

When Louise and Babs returned without shopping bags, I knew something was afoot. Babs hurried to her husband and hauled him out of the dining room where we had been eating steamed clams together. The manic gleam in Louise's eyes set my heart racing. It was as though she were holding her breath, suppressing a giant shout. I can still feel her shaky, wet hand as she sat down next to me and broke the news.

"We're going to have a baby!"

The way a man reacts to this news reveals everything a woman needs to know about his feelings for her. I stood up, wobbled, and said, "I think I'm going to faint." Louise took this as an expression of joy, when, in fact, it was nauseated dread. She rose on tiptoe, threw her arms around my neck, and stippled me with teeny kisses.

She said, "And the best part is, my mom isn't mad at all! She doesn't even care how soon we get married, as long as it's before the baby comes."

I don't remember much between then and our wedding at the Plaza, except that a few nights before the ceremony, I walked the frozen beach at midnight. Using a can of lighter fluid I had brought with me, I started a fire into which I dropped my European journal. There was no place in my new life for its erotic whimsy and stark candor.

Oh, yes, one more memory from the time, of the evening Bastard Bill and I shared a limousine to my stag party at Peter Luger. As we crossed the bridge, he lit up a brown cigarette and confessed that while he had no doubt that I was going to make it as a novelist, he would feel more comfortable if he knew, before releasing to me and Louise a sizable portion of her trust, that I was holding down a solid nine-to-five job.

Stunned, I muttered something amenable.

"Glad to hear it, Mal." He leaned over and slapped me on the knee. "I'll set it up."

♦   ♦   ♦   ♦   ♦

Prostate a fiery walnut. Lower back sore and stiff. Bowels jammed. Stress, no doubt. My phone never rings. It's Sunday night. What the hell's taking Nora so long? We have no plans until Friday afternoon, but surely when she sees my phone number scrawled on the bottom of her birthday card, she'll call as soon as she has finished reading.

◆　◆　◆　◆　◆

A fine, upstanding fellow keeps a daily diary, but every New Year's Eve he tosses it into the fire, so that his wife and kids will never know his secrets. A few days after his fiftieth Christmas, he drops dead of a heart attack. His brother, following old instructions, rushes over and removes the diary from its hiding place. That night, he sits in front of a roaring fire with the book on his lap. He was told to destroy it without looking inside. He cannot do it. He must know his brother. He opens the book and the terrible things he discovers inside are the novel. Best idea I've had yet. I must explore it.

◆　◆　◆　◆　◆

Chuck looks so inert by the fire that I will not rouse him. I wonder if it is selfish to take him with me. Maybe I ought to let him live out his final years in the only home he has ever known.

◆　◆　◆　◆　◆

My offer on the apartment was accepted today, which is not surprising given that I met the asking price. Many would say that what I did was foolish, but if, working at the magazine, I learned anything about money, it's that peace of mind is priceless. If I had lost the place trying merely to save a buck, I would have been inconsolable.

◆ ◆ ◆ ◆ ◆

Nelson Algren said that it is impossible to be a creative writer in this country without being a loser. Does he mean that our country devalues writers to such an extent that they are excluded from the American Dream, or that only those excluded from the American Dream have the objectivity to become writers? If I am ever lucky enough to be quoted at length in the media about art and culture, I will be crystal-clear in my pronouncements. I will leave obliquity and mystification to the philosophers and critics.

◆ ◆ ◆ ◆ ◆

Nothing from Nora yet. Did she miss my phone number at the bottom of the card? Impossible. I even drew an arrow to it.

◆ ◆ ◆ ◆ ◆

With Louise ten feet away, I called in sick today to the magazine. Too depressed to board the train. Her eyes kept darting to me. It occurred to me that she might know I have no job. If so, my little charade must have been profoundly upsetting to her.

◆ ◆ ◆ ◆ ◆

Remember when there was such a thing as daytime TV? Home sick, you could sink into it like a swamp. Now, with 800 channels, it doesn't exist.

◆ ◆ ◆ ◆ ◆

During a cigarette break, Big Peg mentioned that her mom in Bangor, Maine, breeds Neapolitan mastiffs and that she is herself a dog nut. She told me all about her Dolly, and I told her all about my Chuck. She said that an Irish setter/white Labrador mix sounded beautiful, and I assured her that he is indeed a fetching creature, pun intended, but that he never lets it go to his head. I explained that his fine character is due to the fact that his parents were not random beasts in heat but were deeply in love and spent almost their entire lives together. Amused, she asked if I really believe that dogs, like humans, benefit from being born to committed parents, and I said yes, even if the parents are brother and sister, and we both laughed. Later I mentioned that Chuck has been listless lately, sleeping a lot, and she asked me what the veterinarian said. I told her that I haven't taken him in yet, because Louise says his sluggishness is just a symptom of age. Peg said it might be worth a visit anyway. I asked her if she would like to walk dogs together sometime and she said sure. Little does she know that this will be our first therapy session.

◆ ◆ ◆ ◆ ◆

No matter what Nora thinks of my prose, her silence is unforgivable. The books were a birthday gift, for Christ's sake! On what planet does etiquette not require at least a thank-you call? The only acceptable excuse is disease. How ironic it would be if she were dying while I sat here gnashing my teeth and cursing her. Maybe "ironic" is the wrong word. Anyway, the point is, her silence is starting to suggest to me that she is not the woman I had believed her to be. Is it possible that my muse is a selfish cunt? I'll rot in hell for

writing that. Forgive me. I'm drunk and weary and paralyzed
with fear. If only the phone would ring!

◆ ◆ ◆ ◆ ◆

I am tempted to call the Salem House, but I'm afraid that I
will discover that Nora is perfectly okay, simply taking her
time with my journals, savoring each and every word. If so,
my neediness will turn her stomach, just as it is turning my
own right now. A woman needs her man to be strong. She
can't help it. Simple biology. Especially the one on whom she
bestows her virginity, which, as Shakespeare said, is the "most
immediate jewel of her soul." Wait, maybe not. I think he was
talking about a woman's reputation. Same idea. I'm unwell.
Must sleep. But how? I read a pamphlet at work that said when
people die of a drug overdose, very often it is not suicide at all,
or even reckless hedonism, just a person under tremendous
duress desperately wanting to sleep.

◆ ◆ ◆ ◆ ◆

Wittgenstein: "Whereof one cannot speak, thereof one must
be silent." I will not call her, no matter what.

◆ ◆ ◆ ◆ ◆

My agony in regard to Nora was so acute this morning that I
actually mentioned it to five different suicide callers. I knew
it was foolish, but I couldn't help it. I pretended that I was
sharing the information only to give them insight into their
own suffering. All but one of the callers saw right through it
and reacted with outrage. How dare I talk about myself? They

hated being robbed of the spotlight even for thirty seconds. I calmed them down fairly quickly, except for one, a belligerent firefighter who asked to speak to my supervisor. I told him I was the supervisor and that if he had a problem with my job performance he should take it up with Albany.

Later, I got a call from a particularly asinine fellow, screaming his lungs out because his girlfriend had walked out on him only a few days after promising that she would stay with him forever. He didn't strike me as depressed in the least, just enraged. I explained to him that lovers lie to each other all the time. What are marital vows but promises never to leave, and yet half the people who make them do leave, often at a sprint. It works the other way too. Some lovers walk out in tears, vowing never to come back, and then return a few days later, bearing flowers and candy.

"You mean, she might come back?" he gasped hopefully, completely missing the point.

"You bet," I replied, just to get him off the phone.

My final call was from a stutterer. I am impatient by nature, so his linguistic snags were pure torture. I practically chewed my lip off trying not to finish his sentences. His problem was that his wife of two years had recently become a high-priced escort, and lying in bed at night, waiting for her to return from work, he wanted to die. I told him there was easy cure.

"Th-th-th-ere is?"

"Yeah, divorce."

We're told not to offer advice, but it seemed so obvious to me. The young masochist did not agree, of course, insisting in excruciating stops and starts that she was his best friend on earth.

I interrupted: "Look, I'll find you a therapist, but if he's worth his salt he's just going to tell you what I'm telling you right now. How can you be happily married to a whore? Who do you think you are? Superman? Buddha? It would drive any sane person crazy, and it sounds like you were troubled to begin with. As for her being your best friend, that's absolute crap. This isn't how friends treat each other. It's how enemies treat each other. She hates your god-damn guts."

Damaged beyond repair, he begged for a shrink, and I gave him one. Depressing call. A waste of breath. I have not slept for more than two hours the past four nights.

◆　◆　◆　◆　◆

Abject morning at the library, fretting, daydreaming, ducking out to smoke, and barely able to read *The Red and the Black*. No one knows more about the warfare of love than Stendhal. He was a master tactician, which I suppose he had to be, given that he was chubby and moon-faced. If he had seen me as I emerged from the revolving door at eleven-thirty, hands trembling, patched with sweat, punching out the number of the Salem House, he would have said: "Don't do it, *mon ami*! Be strong! You will lose all advantage!" But I no longer cared about winning and losing. I wanted only to put an end to the waiting. Rhodes answered. He said that Nora was with a customer, and that she would call me back at her earliest convenience.

When Nora had not called me back before my three o'clock training appointment, I broke club rules and tucked my phone into the waist of my sweatpants. Ten minutes later, as Archie stretched me on a big blue plastic ball, it vibrated. Startled, I rolled off and landed hard on my face. I was so embarrassed that I picked up the call without checking to see who it was. It was Louise. Carmen was about to leave for the supermarket and she needed to know: for Saturday's barbecue, cole slaw, macaroni salad, potato salad, or some combination of the three? I said all three sounded great. She detected something strange in my tone. I should have just told her where I was, but lying has become so automatic these days that I said I was at my desk, looking over ad placements. This gave her license to call me back, which she did, three minutes later: "Beer in cans or bottles?" And then two minutes later: "All-beef or turkey dogs or both?" Archie wanted to strangle me, as did everyone else within earshot, and so I was forced to power down the phone, cutting off my lifeline to Nora.

When the session was over, I dashed out and, sure enough, I had received a new voice message. My heart pounded as I dialed. The moment of truth was upon me. Louise again, with an urgent question about buns: "Sesame or plain?" I called her back and screamed "Both! Let's live it up!" Her voice trembled with feeling: "I'm sorry to keep bothering you. I just want it to be a wonderful day for you and the girls." No one has the power to make me feel worse about myself. On the way to Grand Central, I stopped and bought her roses, but by accident left them on the train.

♦   ♦   ♦   ♦   ♦

I am smoking so much tonight that Chuck whimpers each time I light up. The phone does not ring.

♦   ♦   ♦   ♦   ♦

Today I drifted into work like a sleepwalker, unshaved and unshowered, speaking only when spoken to. A mother called, worried about her son who had vandalized Rockland Cemetery last night in an attempt to dig up the body of his best friend who'd died in a motorcycle crash. He wanted to switch places with him. Adding to the mother's distress is that the accident was two years ago, and her son knows perfectly well that he was cremated. I offered her what consolation I could, but I was just going through the motions.

My next call was from a woman who underwent, all in one day, liposuction, a tummy tuck, and a boob job, and yet is still unhappy.

"Wait," I said, "let me get this straight. You had a doctor cut holes in your thighs and suction the fat out, slit open your midriff, yank it tight, and sew it back together again, and jam plastic bags full of saltwater into your boobs, and you aren't any happier? How is such a thing possible?"

Dead silence.

I continued: "Of course you don't feel better. The problem isn't your looks. It never was. It's your head. Fix that and you might not be overjoyed with how you look, but at least you'll be content. Which is more than anyone has a right to expect on this sad, dirty globe."

She hung up on me.

Before I inflicted any more harm, I poked my head into Henry's office and told him I did not feel well and needed to go home.

"Okay!" he said brightly, without looking up from his *Sports Illustrated*.

I drove around for an hour with the air conditioning blasting in my face. When I finally got home, it took Louise only a split second to pick up my mood. Believing that she was the cause of it, she became frantic, growing more and more obsessed with the barbecue. When I barked that it wouldn't be the end of the world if we ran out of plastic cups and had to use paper ones, she fell apart. I followed her upstairs, but she slammed and locked the bedroom door in my face.

"Who are you?" she screamed. "I don't even know you!"

♦ ♦ ♦ ♦ ♦

Is every Catholic, deep down, a masochist or a sadist or both?

♦ ♦ ♦ ♦ ♦

Friday at last! Lunch with Nora. I am rattling into the heart of the city. The pain has been so intense that I no longer feel it. I am actually filled with pride now that I made it through. The bravest are those who dare to love.

♦ ♦ ♦ ♦ ♦

Just left Nora. I am riding the subway to God knows where. No words to describe what just happened. Struggling to compass it.

♦ ♦ ♦ ♦ ♦

Oscar Wilde called himself the Lord of Language, but then lamented that he could not find words to express grief at his mother's death. The distrust of words that can only be felt by he who has mastered them. Or is it him? I never get this one right.

♦ ♦ ♦ ♦ ♦

Almost six hours on the subway. I am heading home.

◆ ◆ ◆ ◆ ◆

Louise waited up for me, unsure whether to be terrified or angry. She asked why I had missed dinner and not picked up my phone all day. I told her that Sid Davis had a second heart event and died. Her face fell, and she opened her long arms to me. Thank God I didn't overdo it in the grief department, as she might have grown suspicious. Sid and I were not all that close. I mean are. Sid is fine. He never had a first, let alone a second heart attack. We haven't socialized with Sid and Staci in years, so as long as Louise doesn't run into one of them, my lie is safe.

◆ ◆ ◆ ◆ ◆

Our Fourth of July barbecue in full swing outside my window. I dislike every guest. Right off the bat, Louise announced Sid's tragic passing, but none of our guests knows him, so it worked out fine. Phew! Okay, I've had my drink. Back to the comedy.

◆ ◆ ◆ ◆ ◆

Today after the barbecue, as the guests trickled home, the girls found me sitting on the jungle gym and asked in near-unison what was the matter with me. Obnoxiousness they were used to, but silence?

Blissfully drunk, I replied: "We can refute assertions, but who can refute silence?"

They were not amused.

"Guess who said it and I'll double your allowance. No idea? Dickens. Yes, and he ought to have known. The dude was a chatterbox. Oh, don't worry about me." I lifted my beer, toasting the setting sun. "I'll find my voice again. And if I don't, who cares? Not you. Your hero once, I'm now just a tiresome creep you barely tolerate. A bit obtuse. At times almost ridiculous. At times, indeed, the fool."

Sarah made a face and insisted that they loved me very much, but that they were worried, that's all. I seemed so unhappy, but I refused to get help. Instead I took it out on everybody else.

"Mommy, you mean."

"Not just her. Everyone."

"Not today."

"No, today you didn't utter a word."

"You're welcome."

"And what's this about Sid Davis being dead? He isn't dead. I saw Marci two days ago."

"Who the hell's Marci?"

"His daughter. We go to school together."

"My Sid Davis doesn't have a daughter. You're obviously thinking of the wrong Sid Davis."

I smiled insouciantly and climbed to a high rung of the jungle gym. They stared at me for a long time, and I stared back. A stubborn stand-off. Finally, they blinked and went inside.

◆   ◆   ◆   ◆   ◆

Fireworks explode far away. I am unmoved by every holiday but Christmas. I still remember Archer's face, just after he turned three, when, opening his presents under the tree, he realized for the first time that Santa Claus brings you exactly what you ask for. Pure wonder. I have never seen anything so beautiful.

◆ ◆ ◆ ◆ ◆

What happened with Nora: I rang the bell. Nora and Rhodes turned and saw me in the glass. My sham grin announced, "Your man of letters has arrived, ready to bask in your adoration." Rhodes darted like a lizard into the back room. Nora reached under the counter for something and walked toward me. She looked pale and gaunt. Black rings under her eyes. Her chin seemed pointier than usual. No sign of warmth in her expression. Maybe I was right and she had been ill, I thought. Then I saw that she was carrying my journals, bound together by a big red rubber band. In an instant, I knew that I had made a terrible mistake. I had given her my journals! Why, why? It was like waking from a terrible nightmare to something far worse. A dozen entries flashed through my mind. Oral sex with a minor. Public masturbation. Fantasies of shredding her hymen. Countless lies. I had given her my journals. Read all about it! Why? What on earth had I been thinking?

She cracked open the door. "Take them and go away."

"But it's Friday."

"Please."

I took the books. "Nora, if something I wrote offended you—"

"I don't judge people, Mr. Poe. I pray for them. I've prayed for you every single night since I read them. I want you to find clarity...happiness...grace. Since you don't believe in God, maybe a psychotherapist might be able to help you."

"How do you know I don't believe in God?"

"It's obvious from your diary. I'm sorry, that was judgmental. I have no right. Good-bye."

I stopped the door with my foot. "You know these

aren't diaries, right? They're journals. A sketch pad for my novel. Most of it's pure invention. I assumed that you would understand that. Evidently—"

"You're lying. I know these books are a confession."

"What're you talking about? No!"

"Then why in the card did you write 'Please accept these intimate confessions?'"

"I did? No! Why would I do that?"

"The whole time I was reading, I thought, Wait, he doesn't believe in God, so who the heck is he confessing to?" She leveled her little green eyes at me. "Good-bye, Malcolm. Please remove your foot from the door."

"You're breaking my heart," I whispered.

"What about mine?"

Her chin trembled, and I saw how crushed she was that her savior had turned out to be a degenerate.

"We can still be together," I begged. "All your dreams can come true. You can quit your job and move in with me. Write poetry all day. I'll buy you a piano. All you have to do is forgive me."

She reflected for a moment, swallowing back her rising tears, and then she said this: "When I was little, my grammy told me that a woman is nothing without a warm heart. I thought that was interesting. It felt true. But then I wondered what a man needs to have. I thought about it for years. I never knew until I read your journals. A man needs courage."

"Are you calling me a coward?"

She mistook my indignation for rage, and it frightened her. She slammed the door hard on my foot. I wrestled my shoe free, and the door crashed shut. She locked it. Rhodes rushed out from the back room. When I saw him reach for the telephone, I hurried away.

◆   ◆   ◆   ◆   ◆

Gay's epitaph: "Life is a jest; and all things show it.
I thought so once; but now I know it."

◆   ◆   ◆   ◆   ◆

I wanted to set down some kind words about my darling wife,
who, sensing my despair, has been bending over backward to
make me happy. Instead, uncharitable thoughts about her tap
tap tap at the back of my brain, and I do not have the strength
of character to banish them, and so I lay down my pen for the
night. A baseball game will relax me.

◆   ◆   ◆   ◆   ◆

A college girl called today who, until a few weeks ago, was
sleeping with her history professor. After she dumped him,
he began to act erratically, and this morning she spotted him
outside her dormitory, wearing only a bathrobe, talking to
the flower beds. She stuck her head out the window, begging
him to come inside, but he told her he didn't have time. He
was on his way to jump into the river and needed to say good-
bye to her tulips first. She called us for help. I took down the
information and, coached by Big Peg, called the local police,
who sent a squad car and an ambulance. They also called the
professor's home and spoke with his wife, who of course had
no idea that his husband had a girlfriend. When the professor
arrived at the hospital, his wife was already there, waiting for
him. She had to be held back by the medics as she attempted
to claw his eyes out.
     When I told Peg how sorry I felt for the guy, my voice

shook. She touched my arm and asked what was wrong. I started to tell her about Nora, but I broke down almost at once, not so much in tears as in growls and moans. She tossed her cigarette, pulled me close, and I fell into her big strong arms. A true bear hug. I thought of Faulkner. Then she whispered that the boss man was coming. I snapped to and cleared my throat as he strode past.

"Get a room," Henry snickered.

◆ ◆ ◆ ◆ ◆

Daniel Webster: "There is no refuge from confession but suicide; and suicide is confession." I am not sure what this means. Is he saying that everything is confession? If so, then everything is not a confession. Why does he obfuscate like this? The first incumbency of an artist is to communicate clearly.

◆ ◆ ◆ ◆ ◆

After being charged for last week's missed session, I was determined not to miss another, no matter how depressed I was. I decided in advance that when Archie asked me why I had not shown up, I would either lie or shut up. He is just a boy, for heaven's sake, only nineteen. In his eyes, I am an entirely different order of human. Methuselah crossed with a redwood riding on a tortoise. The last thing he needs to hear are the complaints of my ancient broken heart.

"Nice of you to drop by," Archie said with a cocky smile. "What the hell happened last week?"

I spilled my guts, babbling on about the most intimate things imaginable. When I was finished, he looked shell shocked.

The best he could manage was: "Well, you know what they say—the best way to get over a woman is to get under another one."

He grinned and bobbed his eyebrows. There it was. The sum total of his wisdom. Out of the mouths of babes come vomit. I told him that I could not imagine finding a better woman than Nora and that I had pretty much resigned myself to a life of loneliness. His face colored slightly, and with a cock of his head he ushered me into the corner near the drinking fountain. I followed him, even though I had a feeling that something unpleasant was about to take place.

"How about Veronica Veronique?" he whispered.

"What do you mean?"

"We're friends now."

"Since when?"

"Last week. She likes you. She'd totally do you."

"How do you know?"

"She told me. Except she's...well, she's pretty expensive."

"Because she orders the surf 'n' turf or because she's a prostitute?

He grinned and bobbed his eyebrows.

"Oh, okay. I get it. What's your cut?"

"What do you mean?"

"What percentage do you get for the new customers you bring her?"

"A third."

I no longer saw in him my lost son, given, miraculously, the gift of extended life. I saw skies dripping fire. Buildings toppling. Mayhem in the streets. Bonfires of books. Plagues of frogs and lice. I deplore this new generation. If this kid had a child with Juliet Hacker, it would come out a shit-eating monkey. If Archer had lived, he would have been different, I know it. He would have made me proud. He would have lived and loved wisely. He would have embodied the best values of Western civilization. He would not have been a pimp.

♦   ♦   ♦   ♦   ♦

I used to tell Archer that when little boys grow up and get bigger than their daddies, most daddies stop hugging and kissing them, but that I never would.

"Even when you're this tall," I'd say, "taller than I am, I'm still going to kiss your neck and tickle your belly and bite your butt."

He'd squeal, "No, Daddy!"

"Oh yeah," I'd say. "Just you wait!"

♦   ♦   ♦   ♦   ♦

Louise, surprised to see me loading Chuck into the car, asked me where I was taking him.

"The vet," I said.

"Mal, we discussed this. He's just getting old."

"I think it might be cancer."

"Now you're including animals in your hypochondria?"

"One of these days one of my paranoid suspicions will be correct. And won't you be embarrassed?"

I drove over to the Memorial Park, where Peg waited with Dolly, who is not the slobbering mastiff I had expected but a preternaturally calm wire-haired fox terrier with a bold black saddle and a sweet buff head. While Chuck sniffed her silly, Peg and I strolled the humid park. She wore cut-off jeans, a commie T-shirt, and big clunky sandals that elevated her to well over six feet. Peg is a strapping beauty, the exact opposite of Nora in every conceivable way. Nora is all soul; Peg is all flesh. Nora is a virgin; Peg is a wanton. Nora is as slender and fragrant as a spring flower; Peg is as wide-hipped and musky as a baby hippo. If I were less superficial, I would probably fall in love with her.

We picked up right where we'd left off at work, except now my grief was well under control. I told her everything, beginning with my wedding day and ending with Nora returning my journals. The epic took two full hours, by which time we were halfway through a pack of cigarettes and a six-pack of beer.

"Okay," I said, "I'm ready."

"For what?"

"Any insights you might have."

"Personal or professional?"

"Both. Either."

"You lack courage? How dare she! You've stayed married for twenty-five years, and now you're going to give up the good life to live alone and write a novel? That takes guts. Nora's the coward. I bet she's never even sucked a cock."

The beer almost came out of my nose as I laughed.

"But, seriously, Mal? I think she might be clinically depressed. With suicidal tendencies."

"Based on what?"

"A thirty-nine-year-old virgin with a history of abuse. Her favorite poem is 'Howl.' You do the math. If you'd hooked up with her, it would have been a busman's holiday. You'd have been talking her off the ledge within no time."

"God, what if you're right? What if she kills herself?"

"Talk about winning the post-break-up."

I laughed again. It felt good to smile. I'm not sure if I agree with Peg's diagnosis, but I sure enjoyed hearing it. We opened a couple more beers, lay on the grass near the war memorial, and now it was her turn to talk. She played basketball in college and would have turned pro if she hadn't blown out a knee. After she graduated, she lived with a male civil rights attorney for three years, and then with a female bread baker for three more. She considers herself a genuine bisexual. She makes love to the person, she said, not the genitals. I love the idea of her naked with another woman, especially if the other woman is as tiny as Nora.

As shadows gathered, Peg gave Chuck a quick layman's examination. Turns out he's chock full of lipoma—soft, benign, painless lumps. A common canine malady, she says. I asked if they should be removed, and she said at Chuck's age that would be ridiculous. She said that for the remainder of Chuck's life, my goal should be to keep him as comfortable and content as possible.

"Might be a good goal for myself," I quipped.

She laughed and ruffled my hair as though I were a little boy. Then she scooped up Dolly and was gone. Best day I've had since the drive to Brooklyn. I listened to Mozart all the way home and even did a bit of conducting.

"You were right," I said to Louise when I walked in. "Just old age."

She asked me if I'd run into Karen at the animal hospital. My heart skipped a beat.

"I saw her, but she was so busy I didn't even say hi."

◆　◆　◆　◆　◆

On our honeymoon, we awoke each morning to the dazzling blue of the Caribbean, but all I saw on the horizon was my future, creeping and billowing like a radioactive cloud. Why had I given in so swiftly to Bastard Bill's demand? I had never worked a real job in my life. I was Kafka not Gregor Samsa, and if I pretended to be the latter, I would wake up a cockroach. Would my new job require that I wear a tie? Shoes that required shining? Would the fluorescent lighting make my hair fall out? Ironically, my worst fear was not even that I would despise the job, but that I would grow to love it, and forget that I had ever been young, brilliant, and ambitious.

I had no one to turn to for consolation or counsel, not even my new wife, because she was overjoyed with my gutless decision, as well as crippled by around-the-clock morning sickness. We spent every day in our suite, leafing through magazines, making love, watching TV, and debating baby names. Only once was Louise well enough even to step foot on the beach, but, embarrassed by the eight pounds she had already gained, she abandoned the idea almost immediately. My only release came at night, after Louise had fallen asleep, when I escaped to the bar.

When we got back to New York, Bill and Babs surprised us with a final wedding gift: a six-bedroom house on four acres.

"No big deal," Bill said. "We just wanted to see you well settled."

"No big deal? How can you say that?"

He frowned. "No tennis court."

'Within a few weeks, Bill had delivered on his promise to find me a job. I lived like a pasha, but each morning I commuted into the city to proofread financial text about which I knew almost nothing and cared even less. I told myself that I was still an artist deep down and that as soon as the baby was born, I would roll up my sleeves and begin my novel. This was nonsense, of course, because, as every parent knows, the first few months after a baby's birth are like a cruel sleep-deprivation experiment. When we realized how tough it was going to be, Louise offered to hire a nurse so that Annie's cries wouldn't wake me up, but I refused. I adored my baby girl and, despite my exhaustion, I considered it a privilege to wake up in the wee hours to give her a bottle. No, even grander than that—a sacrament.

The only real casualties of fatherhood, then, were my literary aspirations. Was this a genuine loss or an imaginary one? After all, between my college graduation and meeting Louise, I had had all the time in the world to write but had never finished a single readable page. Would I have broken through in time? Found my voice? I'll never know. Instead of starting a novel, I began a journal, but not like the one I had kept in Europe. This was a baby book, beginning with the moment of Annie's birth, and filled with careful, loving observations of her introduction to the planet. With the birth of each baby, I began a new book, so by the time they were all in school, I had four going all at once.

These books brought me much pleasure, not only in the writing of them but also because they enabled me to relive again and again the charms and wonders of new fatherhood. First teeth, first steps, first words. By the time Archer was killed and I gave up the tradition, I had filled fifteen volumes.

One Christmas morning, I gave each girl her journals to keep. They had not even known they existed. Annie, the eldest, finished reading hers first. She came downstairs, sniffling, chin trembling, and told me it was the best gift she had ever received. I thought to myself: Maybe I am a writer, after all.

◆ ◆ ◆ ◆ ◆

D.H. Lawrence: "I want love that is like sleep, like being born again, vulnerable as a baby that just comes into the world.

◆ ◆ ◆ ◆ ◆

Scott Spencer: "It was a pure father's love, effortless and insane."

◆ ◆ ◆ ◆ ◆

Just booked a colonoscopy, which the first two doctors I called insisted that I did not need. The third must be building a new wing on his house because he leapt at the gig. I don't understand why the medical establishment is so stingy with these lifesaving procedures. If scopes were dangerous, I would understand completely, but the number of infections and deaths is almost infinitesimal.

◆ ◆ ◆ ◆ ◆

Party at Alton and Jo Copley's. Tense moment when a friend of theirs, a fork-tongued, duck-footed hedge fund manager named Don Leopold, cited an article in this month's *Investors Monthly* called "Bailout Fallout." He begged to differ with me on a few points, but since I haven't read a copy of the magazine since my dismissal, it was impossible for me to comment. In order to conceal the truth, I told him I never talked shop at social occasions. A half dozen guests with whom I have talked shop at numerous social occasions laughed and called me a dirty rotten liar. I said it was a *new* rule. This silenced everyone but dumb-ass Leopold, who wouldn't let up. I gently demurred each time, wearing an enlightened smile. As soon as she got me alone, Louise kissed me on the lips and thanked me for not making a scene.

The rest of the night I watched our hosts' tattooed sons shoot pool. I absorbed many details that will be invaluable if I ever write a book about this new lost generation. These boys were not revolting in the way Archie is. They were revolting in a different way. They wore ski caps indoors and spoke in monosyllables. Worse, they were incapable of going two minutes without glancing at their phones. I asked myself if I and my friends were similarly distracted at their age. The answer was no. For better or worse, we actually inhabited time and space and were never more fiercely present than when we played games.

◆　◆　◆　◆　◆

At work today a female caller confided that she likes to cram cereal into her aroused vagina in order to hear the snap crackle pop. I think she expected me either to be turned on or scandalized. Instead I called her a crazy pig and slammed the phone down. Peg invited me outside for a smoke. Once I was puffing away, she said that what I had just done was a really big deal. I told her that I wasn't coping well with the breakup and that I was scared to death of living alone. She said she was very sorry to hear this, but that didn't make it okay for me to take it out on our customers.

"Are you going to tell Henry?" I asked.

"I don't have to. He heard you. Everyone did."

I told her that I wasn't temperamentally suited to the job, and as I would have to leave anyway when I moved to the city, maybe this was as good a time as any for me to quit. She said that she was pleased I had come to this conclusion on my own, which means, I suppose, that I was about to be fired. She patted me on the back and walked me into Glover's office, where I tendered my resignation effective immediately. He did not conceal his relief.

♦ ♦ ♦ ♦ ♦

Before you drive yourself toward a great solitude, you'd better have something inside you. To surround yourself with desert and have only desert inside will drive you mad. You must have riches in your depths in order to bear the empty, wide, distractionless days ahead. You must have built campsites, homesteads, hamlets, and cities in your imagination. Only then will you be able to face the silent nights, the days with no agenda, the years that pass seamless into the next. So, brave artist, before you turn your back on the world's spectacle and begin your life's work, gather your abundance!

♦ ♦ ♦ ♦ ♦

Nora brought up an interesting point. To whom am I confessing? I will ask this question of Chuck.

♦ ♦ ♦ ♦ ♦

I asked him, and he did not stir. I will ask again, louder.

♦ ♦ ♦ ♦ ♦

Nothing. I think, on top of everything else, he is going deaf. Unless he is just tuning me out because I am drunk and tiresome.

◆ ◆ ◆ ◆ ◆

Yesterday Louise's pal Greg Gardner flew home to Phoenix, Arizona, for his father's seventieth birthday party. Ellie stayed behind with their troll baby. After the party, held at a local restaurant, Greg offered his two favorite nephews a ride home in his hot-shit rented sports car. On the way, they were T-boned by a teenage drunk driver. The drunk driver and both of Greg's nephews were killed instantly. Greg is in critical condition with internal bleeding and multiple fractures. Louise is over at Ellie's apartment right now, helping her pack.

Something is clearly wrong with me. My first thought when I heard the tragic news was that Ellie might be back on the market soon, and that she is so cute I might be willing to adopt her ugly son. I must begin therapy as soon as possible.

◆ ◆ ◆ ◆ ◆

Just hung up with Jack Trippet. My meeting with the co-op board is set for Monday. He told me not to be afraid.

◆ ◆ ◆ ◆ ◆

I broke it to Archie that I no longer want to train with him. Too expensive. He said that when it comes to training, he has learned that it is never the money that makes people give up. It's always just an excuse, masking a deeper reason. I told him he was right. The deeper reason is that every time I see him I imagine my dead son all grown up and pimping on the side, and it makes me want to poke out his fucking eyes.

◆ ◆ ◆ ◆ ◆

A dunce of days, I strive to be a scholar of years. I am fast approaching the age where if a man is not wise he is absolutely nothing. A few minutes ago, I noticed that the skin on the flesh between my thumb and index finger has changed. It is crepe paper now. Old-man skin. When I saw it I thought at once of my grandfather. Why is it such a shock to be on the cusp of old age? My entire generation is in denial about time. We think that because we are not the soulless husks our grandparents were, we are somehow still young and viable. Boy, are we all in for a surprise when Death comes a-calling.

♦   ♦   ♦   ♦   ♦

A library whisper: "I mean, it's cool to talk during sex if it's, like, you know, hot, dirty stuff, but with him it's just random junk." I do this with Louise sometimes. Once, during sex, I asked if she had seen my snow shovel anywhere.

♦   ♦   ♦   ♦   ♦

Back from the doctor. My intestinal tract is clean as a whistle. No polyps, no cancer. A few old hemorrhoids is all. I am grateful. Now if only my prostate would stop aching. Is there nothing out there to douse the flaming walnut? I asked the doctor and he said, "Sorry, I don't do wee-wees." Funny guy. He told me the story of an old duffer whose prostate hurt so badly that he decided since he never got laid anyway he might as well get the damn thing removed. He had the operation, but even with the gland gone, the pain didn't subside. This underscores the fact that the area in question is a mysterious nexus of multiple nerve endings. Imagine a third-world slum, where thousand of phone and power lines hang from poles in scary, chaotic hives. That's a man's pelvic floor. His crux. Add a little sexual shame, born of a mother who walked around the house stark naked until her son threatened her with murder, and you get an idea of why mine has throbbed since I was thirty.

♦   ♦   ♦   ♦   ♦

Friday 11:35 a.m. Normally, five minutes from now, I would walk over to the Salem House with a smile in my heart. (Rancid cliché.) I wonder what would happen if I pretended that Nora had never rejected me, simply rang the bell, and, when she appeared, said, "Hey, gorgeous, let's eat."

♦   ♦   ♦   ♦   ♦

I did it. I walked over there. When I did not see Nora inside, I asked where she was. Rhodes told me that she was on vacation and that if I did not step away from the door he would call the police. I told him that the customer is always right and there was no need to threaten me. He said that my very presence was a threat.

"Why?" I shouted. "Because I haven't shaved?"

He threw a hand on his hip. "Or bathed, from the looks of you."

"You know what you are, Rhodes? The groom on a gay wedding cake. You ought to be teaching ballroom dancing in Iowa somewhere."

The look on his face was priceless.

I admit that my mental state has taken a toll on my grooming standards, but that hardly makes me a public nuisance. Fuck him. All that matters is Nora. She is not on vacation. She can't afford a vacation. Is she at home, heartbroken? Sick? I would rush to her side right now, but I don't know where she lives! Driving to her brownstone that afternoon, I was having so much fun that I merely followed instructions and paid no attention to where I was going.

♦ ♦ ♦ ♦ ♦

When the front door slammed and Annie walked in, carrying her suitcase, Louise burst out crying at the happy surprise. While they hugged and kissed and hugged some more, I stood there grinning like an idiot, arms outstretched. It went on for so long, I didn't know where to put my hands. As much as I adore Annie, I knew this was no impulse visit. Annie has an attorney's mind. She is immune to caprice.

While Carmen shoveled Annie full of scrambled eggs, I asked her the sort of questions a doting daddy is supposed to ask of his far-flung first-born. I asked about her beloved mate and the progress of "Fisch in a Barrel." I barely heard her replies. My heart raced as I wondered, What is she doing home? Pregnant? Engaged? Married? Breast cancer?

Hours later, Louise suggested lunch at the Marina Club. Louise thinks I loathe the place because of the raw veal chop they served me a few years ago, but it's actually because the Craters are lifelong members and the sight of them in Bermuda shorts makes me soul-sick. Annie loves the club's seafood salad, however, so the next thing I knew we were rumbling over the bridge in Louise's big Jag. Annie reached back and raked her fingernails through my stubble.

"Your idea or Mom's?" she asked.

"No one's. I've just been lazy. Should I keep it?"

"Does it bother Mom when you kiss?"

I found Louise's sad eyes in the rearview.

"Nope," she said. "I love it. It's sexy."

As the food arrived, the Craters toddled past, right on cue. Earl with his huge gut, eczema, and blanched legs. Estelle with her hacking cough and shaky hands. Somehow we went unnoticed. No sooner had I exhaled my relief than Louise popped over to their table for some spunky chitchat. What on earth did they talk about for ten minutes? Did Louise ask how their daughter was doing (the one who killed our son), or did she stick to trivial matters like liver disease and adult diapers?

Annie and I read our menus in silence. Her black eyes were jumpy and troubled. She knew that I knew she had a good reason for being here. I could see the wheels turning in her pretty head as she struggled to find the right words to explain.

Retaking her seat, Louise murmured, "Poor things."

I replied, "Bullshit. I'm gonna save my sympathy for people who play no willful role in their own demise. Like African babies. The Craters choose gin. African babies don't choose malaria."

"And you choose Scotch!" Annie barked. "How is that any better?"

I might have said something back, but her eyes were so filled with feeling that I was stopped cold. But what feeling? Not anger. I think it was fear. Did she actually think I wasn't in control of my drinking? In that instant I wished I could have asked Louise to leave the table so that I might explain to Annie the nightmare of the past two weeks.

Back home, just as I was ready to flop into much-needed oblivion, Annie bounded down the stairs in shorts, suggesting a run along the river, just the two of us. I said no in a dozen amusing ways, but she went right on insisting. Finally, she grabbed my hand and hauled me up. "Mom says you've got

a trainer now. Come on, old geezer, show me what you got."
When I returned in my sweats, she laughed and said: "Looks
like he's been training you to eat pasta and ice cream."

The run wasn't nearly as torturous as I had expected. She
let me walk whenever I needed to, which was about every
fifty feet. We talked about Karen, i.e., her summer job at
the animal hospital, her feelings about starting college, and
her incipient lesbianism. Even though I live with her, Annie
knows much more about Karen than I do. They speak, text,
and tweet all day, whereas if I ran into Karen's room with my
clothes and hair on fire, it would be a full ten seconds before
she removed her ear buds and said, "What is it now?" Walking
the last quarter mile, I fell silent, creating space for Annie to
come clean about her visit, but she never did.

Louise and Annie, both weight-conscious, decided to
skip dinner and eat popcorn in front of the TV. From among
the movies that Karen had ordered this week, Louise chose
one of her all-time favorites, and my all-time least favorite,
Bringing Up Baby. Annie had never seen it and was excited by
the cast. I bulged my eyes at her, trying to warn her, but she
didn't see me.

While Louise and Annie munched and giggled, I stared
stone-faced at the frantic nonsense playing out on the screen.
I inwardly seethed, wondering how Louise could have done
this to me. Did she really hate me that much? Then it occurred
to me that she might have forgotten how much I disliked the
film. Or maybe I'd never told her. Often in a long marriage
you think you've said something repeatedly that, in fact,
you've never uttered, and just as often you think you've never
said something that you've said three times just that morning.

By the time the credits rolled, I was craving a cocktail,
three cigarettes, and some quality time alone. As I rose, Annie

abruptly plucked an unmarked disc from her purse.

"Ta-da!"

"What is it?" Louise asked, getting right to the point.

"The world premiere of 'Fisch in a Barrel,'" I said.

"How did you know?" Annie cried.

"Lucky guess."

"It's only a rough cut."

"I feel so privileged," Louise cooed.

Annie stared at me, waiting for me to say something sardonic and cruel. Instead, I gave her a smile that could go either way.

Because Annie values her mother's critical judgment even less than I do, when she laid the disc in Louise's hand and not mine, I knew in a flash the reason for her visit: money.

We watched the entire rough cut, which, though it was indeed rough, was hardly cut at all. It was intended to be around twenty-five minutes. It ran forty-seven. Rather than go overboard in my critique, revealing more about myself than about the film, I will limit myself to five adjectives: sentimental, putrid, dreary, dumb, and pretentious. Okay, five more: obvious, manipulative, twee, self-indulgent, and horrendous. Louise's critique amounted to a single adjective repeated over and over again like a sorority cheer: "Adorable! Adorable! Adorable!"

I muttered: "And Pol Pot was puckish."

"Stop it!" Annie snapped.

"No fighting," Louise begged.

"So how much of your mom's hard-inherited cash does the boy genius need to finish his masterpiece?" I asked.

Annie tried to hide her surprise. "Twelve thousand. And then when it gets into festivals, a few thousand more for travel expenses."

"You mean *if* it gets into festivals."

"I mean when."

Our eyes locked.

Mine said, "Your boyfriend's film is crap."

Hers said, "Joshua is a born artist who makes love to me nightly. You are a born editor who will be dead in no time."

Louise scampered upstairs. Annie waited, legs and arms crossed, her smile proud and defiant. Already defeated, I picked at one of my thumbs, as though inspecting an overgrown cuticle. The front door slammed. Karen entered, exhausted from her day of giving laxatives to dogs and milking the ass glands of iguanas. When she learned that she had missed the world premiere of her sister's movie, she snatched the disc from the machine and flew upstairs. A minute later Louise descended, blowing on a freshly signed check for twenty-five thousand dollars. She'd thrown in extra so the young filmmakers could travel in style. I would have bet anything that Karen would've hate "Fisch" as much as I did, but when I went to kiss Louise good night, I heard her in her bedroom, laughing her fool head off. Is mine the last consciousness on earth not to have been raped by aliens?

◆ ◆ ◆ ◆ ◆

A wheelchair-bound tech genius, using only his prodigious computer skills, destroys his daughter's boyfriend without ever leaving his desk.

◆ ◆ ◆ ◆ ◆

Thank God for this room and the merciful oblivion that reigns after midnight.

◆   ◆   ◆   ◆   ◆

Five ancient gnomes just trundled past me into the meeting room. These are the board members who will decide my fate. They did not grace me with so much as a glance. Jack Trippet says the most important thing is to relax, be myself, and tell the truth. I told him if I could do that, I'd be sitting on a mountaintop in Nepal.

◆   ◆   ◆   ◆   ◆

Inquisition over. It seems that when one of the board members called the magazine to confirm my employment, they were told that I had retired six months ago. This raised a red flag, of course, as it contradicted my application, which said that I still worked there. After going through my finances with a fine-toothed comb, their accountant determined that, without some outside assistance, I could not be relied upon, in years to come, to make my monthly maintenance fees. This put me in a nasty bind, the only escape from which was disclosure of the fact that I was married to a wealthy woman and that we were about to get divorced. I explained that I had no intention of making off with the huge chunk of Louise's fortune to which I'm legally entitled, but that I would certainly never have to worry about money for as long as I lived.

Just my luck, four of the five board members were women. They made no effort to hide their disdain for me. The lone male, clearly envious of my good fortune, asked me with a leer just how much I "expected to clear."

"Around ten million. So, you see, my having retired is hardly relevant to this discussion."

A gargoyle wearing a crooked auburn wig growled: "But

lying is. Lying's super fucking relevant."

The others smiled nervously.

I sincerely apologized for lying and explained that being forced into retirement was so humiliating that I hadn't even told my wife about it.

Her eyes bugged freakishly: "But she knows now, right?"

"No, which is why I concealed it from you. It didn't seem right that you should know more about my personal life than she does. But just so you don't think I'm a total deadbeat, I want you to know that I do have a job. I work at a suicide help line. The money isn't great, but the work is terribly meaningful."

It suddenly occurred to me that they might call the help line to check up on me, catching me not just in another lie but in an identical one, so I raced ahead, speaking from the heart:

"Honestly, you'll never find a better tenant than I am. I keep to myself, I have no girlfriend, and as it's only human nature to take sides, I doubt my daughters will want to see me after the divorce. At least for a few years. So I'll be all alone, working on my book. You won't even hear the click of computer keys, because I write longhand."

Was this enough to make up for my deceit? I have no idea. Neither does Jack, who was very upset with me when I told him what happened. He says the only things working in my favor are the magnitude of Louise's fortune and the fact that perfect applicants are few and far between.

◆　◆　◆　◆　◆

Saturday we are off to Nantucket for two weeks. I will miss this wonderful reading room. As big as my dreams. It has been my sanctuary, my temple, my hallowed ground, where each day I've worshiped at my teetering totem pole of books. Last night I bit my mouth guard in two while I slept, so I suppose this vacation, the last I will ever take with my family, could not have come at a better time.

◆ ◆ ◆ ◆ ◆

Nora is still absent from work. It breaks my heart to imagine her suffering alone. I approached Rhodes at closing time to ask about her, but he sprinted down the block to evade me. He ran like a girl, arms flailing, hands in scoops. I needed a good laugh. Maybe If I drive around Brooklyn, I will remember where Nora lives. If only I had paid more attention when I drove there.

◆ ◆ ◆ ◆ ◆

Louise took Karen on a shopping spree today, although it was hardly the extravaganza that would have taken place had it been either of her two sisters. Karen's wardrobe consists mostly of jeans, T-shirts, sweat socks, boots, and misshapen sweaters. Still, it's a timeless ritual before a kid starts college, so she did not put up much of a fight and came back bearing many shopping bags. In her innocent, uneasy smile, I detected a child's pure love for her mommy mingled with a touch of regret that she could not please her by being more of a girly-girl.

Along these lines, Karen and her new college roommate Athena, the granddaughter of a Greek shipping tycoon, have been assigned to a riot-proof dormitory from the 1970s, which is said to be a maze of dead-ends and M.C. Escher staircases. They talked on the phone last week to decide who was going to bring the fridge/microwave/printer. Assessing Athena's Facebook friends, her favorite books and films, and her long list of fan sites, Karen has come to the conclusion that Athena is a lesbian. Karen says that this makes her a little bit uncomfortable. She has nothing against lesbians, she insists, but to share a bathroom with one is kind of scary. I almost burst out laughing. Mankind's capacity for denial is breathtaking.

♦   ♦   ♦   ♦   ♦

I can tell that Louise is scared to death of Karen's moving out, because it condemns her to endless years cooped up with me. Boy, is she in for a shock. I wonder if she will go on living here after I am gone, or if she will also move into the City. She is only forty-five and still somewhat attractive. And of course she is rich. Will I be jealous when she takes her first lover?

♦   ♦   ♦   ♦   ♦

No.

♦   ♦   ♦   ♦   ♦

Jack Trippet called. The board unanimously rejected me. One member—he refused to divulge which, but I have a hunch it was the winged gremlin in the auburn wig—thinks I am mentally ill and could prove harmful to myself and/or others. Since she has no idea of the ordeal I just went through with Nora, this does not surprise or offend me. It was simply not meant to be. I will rent.

♦ ♦ ♦ ♦ ♦

It took me five solid hours of driving in circles before I found
Nora's brownstone. I rang the front bell and no one came, but
then I saw a little old lady wobbling toward me, so bent over
from scoliosis that she stared directly at her witchy shoes.
Nora's racist landlady. She did not even know I was waiting
for her until she was about three feet away and saw my legs.
She gasped and glanced up, expecting, no doubt, to see a
black face and the barrel of a gun. I sat down on the stoop and
asked gently if I might speak to Nora Woodling. She said that
that was impossible. Nora was in the hospital.

"Why, what's the matter with her?"

"None of your business. I don't know you."

"Ma'am, please you don't have to—"

"I'll do whatever I want! Outta my way!"

After she had wobbled inside and slammed the door,
I dialed the Salem House. I told Rhodes where I was and
what I had just learned. I begged him to tell me what was
wrong with Nora. I must have sounded desperate, because
his heart budged. He said that she had been suffering from
violent mood swings and that she had checked herself in for
observation and to get her medication changed. She hadn't
expected to stay long, but her condition took an almost
immediate turn for the worse. Now there was no telling how
long it would be. I pretended that I had not been thrown for a
loop. I mentioned casually that I wanted to send her flowers.
Which hospital was she in? He said politely that he was not
at liberty to divulge that, but that he would be happy to take
flowers to her if I had them delivered to the shop.

♦ ♦ ♦ ♦ ♦

How did Peg know that Nora was mentally ill without even meeting her? And how did I miss it? If I hadn't been so self-absorbed, I might have helped Nora instead of making things worse. Surely she was in no condition to read my journals. I shudder when I think of her reading those vivid descriptions of my taking her virginity.

♦ ♦ ♦ ♦ ♦

Today on the train, Fred Samuelson, as dapper and urbane as ever, told me that from time to time all happily married people fear that they've married the wrong person. They come to this conclusion because they have certain friends they enjoy more than they do their own spouses. They feel more relaxed, more *themselves*, with these people, and fret that their lives would have been better if they had married one of them instead. Fred says this is poppycock, because the reason we picked our spouses in the first place and that we're still with them after all these years is that they are our complements, our balance, the gravity that keeps us tethered to reality and to the cruel passage of time. To marry someone just like yourself is redundant and, in the end, unsustainable. His insights both cheered and frightened me. What if life without Louise is not as I imagine it to be? What if I miss her, and she won't take me back?

♦ ♦ ♦ ♦ ♦

When I walked in, Chuck walked around the couch with just the tip of his tail aloft and a watery look in his eye that said, "Sorry, Dad, but I have bad news for you." I checked his gums and they were as white as chalk. I bundled him into the backseat of my car just as Louise drove up. She read the situation at once and jumped in next to me.

We sped to the clinic, where, as luck would have it, Karen was on duty. With her help, Chuck was admitted at once. After a forty-minute wait, during which Louise laid her head on my shoulder, a nurse led us into a private room, where Dr. Skobel waited, holding a blood-filled vial.

"I drew this from his abdomen," he said. "Looks like cancer. Hang tight, we'll know soon enough."

We waited another twenty minutes before Skobel returned, this time with Karen. The ultrasound showed that Chuck's cancerous spleen was bleeding into his lungs. Louise burst out crying. Karen embraced her, and soon she was crying too. Skobel said that it would be best to put Chuck down immediately. Louise reached over and squeezed my biceps so hard that I had to break her grip.

I said to the doctor: "What if we took him home to die? Would that be all right?"

He thought about it and said, "Fine, just as long as you promise to bring him back the moment he starts to fail."

"How long will that be, do you think?"

"A few days at most."

Sarah and Annie, not big animal lovers, will go on ahead to Nantucket alone. Karen will stay with us until the bitter end. She and Louise are both wrecks. I have not cried yet, which is surprising given that Chuck is as much my dog as theirs. I used to cry all the time, but rarely in later years.

♦　♦　♦　♦　♦

Six-month checkup with Dr. Halperin. The oral hygienist who almost murdered me has been replaced by a chubby

Jamaican who is vastly more competent than her predecessor but who stinks of hair products. Even though it was just a light cleaning this time, I requested gas. I so badly crave escape. It was lovely. I floated in the ether, no space creatures in sight. I understood for the first time that human existence is entirely insubstantial. Nothing to worry one's pretty little head over. It's somewhere between a dream and a memory, and when you die it all vanishes into nothing. No loss, really, because it was never real in the first place.

As I gradually came to, I realized that I was listening to the rock band Bread, whose music, even under the paranoia of nitrous oxide, is utterly benign. It filled me with nostalgia for high school make-out sessions when I would spend two hours sucking a girl's tongue and rubbing her mound over her jeans, and never once think to ask for anything in return.

When I opened my eyes, Dr. Halperin was standing over me with a big forced smile. I smiled back, then reached into my pocket and handed him my broken mouth guard. He said he would be happy to replace it free of charge. He's still terrified that I'm going to sue him. To put his mind to rest, I told him that I was disappointed I had not overdosed again, that it was the highpoint of my spiritual life, and that I would give anything to repeat it. He thought I might be joking, so he laughed.

♦ ♦ ♦ ♦ ♦

We knew the end was near last night. Chuck had eaten almost nothing since we'd brought him home, and he hadn't lifted his head from the sheepskin all day. His breathing was fast and raspy. His eyes were closed almost all the time, and when they opened they were filled with fear. We said our goodbyes after midnight. We laughed, looked at old photos, and thanked him for being such an incredible friend. His love was truly unconditional. I know it sounds ridiculous, but I aspire to be his equal.

We took him to the clinic the minute it opened. The end was heartbreaking. Seventy pounds of love closing its eyes for the last time. I tried so hard to take in every detail because I knew we were going to be leaving without him. Even as they injected him, and his life slipped away, I did not shed a tear.

♦ ♦ ♦ ♦ ♦

For the past ten years, whenever I left the room Chuck would turn his head to look for me, and when I came back in he would wag his tail. He was the only one in the family who genuinely liked me, I think.

♦ ♦ ♦ ♦ ♦

Tony Mazzocco once mentioned an "exit bag" and everyone laughed. I had no idea what he was talking about. He explained that it is the latest in unassisted suicide—an airtight bag equipped with a handy switch that releases helium. Slip it over your head and boom. No muss, no fuss.

♦ ♦ ♦ ♦ ♦

I made love to Louise just now, but I felt guilty the whole time because I knew it was for the last time.

♦ ♦ ♦ ♦ ♦

Dear God. How do I even begin? The inevitable scene finally arrived. It was so much worse than I imagined. I need a drink. I keep looking to the floor for sympathy, forgetting that it is dead and gone.

◆ ◆ ◆ ◆ ◆

Out of nowhere, sitting over lunch, Louise began to question me about my recent erratic behavior. For some reason, I told her the truth. I said that I was miserable in our marriage and had been for years. She said that she knew that. I told her that I intended to move out the day after we delivered Karen to Brown. She said that she would not put up a fight. I asked her if we could remain friends. She said that she loved me very much and didn't see why not. We stared at each other. Eyes dry. Was that it? This is how it ends, without so much as a whimper?

Louise rose to put away the orange juice. I noticed that her hand was trembling. "Why didn't you tell me Doug fired you?"

So it was not finished. Not by a long shot.

"How did you know?"

"Iris told me. Right after it happened. I got a few calls, actually."

"And you just let me not talk about it?"

"I didn't want to embarrass you. I thought you'd tell me after a few days. But then more and more time went by. I didn't know what to do. I assumed you were having an affair. It's been terrible, waiting for you to tell me the truth."

"The girls know too?"

"Of course. They were really mad at first. Now, it's more curiosity. They're desperate to know where you go with your briefcase every morning."

"The library."

She looked more amused than anything else. "Really?"

"Yes, really. I'm working on a novel."

"Oh. Okay. Well, that's wonderful."

"Don't patronize me. Like you have any respect for my work."

She mustered as much sweetness as she could find. "How could I respect it? Or disrespect it? You've never shown me any of it."

My reply was angrier than I intended. "You hated that I wanted to be a novelist. You couldn't wait to trap me in an office. You knew it the whole time, didn't you? You knew your father would never let you marry me unless I had a job. I still remember the smile on your face when I told you about *Investors Monthly*."

"You seemed so happy about it."

"Well, I wasn't! I hate that fucking place! I've hated it for twenty-five years! And now I'm alive again! The way I was before I met you!"

My voice cracked. I started to cry, but I stopped myself just in time.

"Sweetheart, I'm sorry. You could have quit whenever you wanted. I never cared whether you worked or not."

I told her I didn't believe her.

She walked over to me, insisting it was true.

For a long time we just sat there, holding hands. I was mostly sulking, wondering why it had taken us so long to have this conversation. It's incredible the things husbands and wives manage not to talk about. I lit up a cigarette, something I never do in her presence. She did not object. So I could have been smoking all these years, too?

Eventually, Louise stopped being strong and patient,

and succumbed to a woman's fate: tears. She said that she was glad I was moving out, because even though she loved me with all her heart, she hated our life together as much as I did. She said that ever since Archer died, there had been no joy. Everything sweet, generous, kind, and fun about me had slowly drained away and never come back. At first she had thought it was simply grief, but then after a few years she had wondered if maybe it was the medication I was taking. When I never returned to my old self, she sought professional help. Her therapist suggested that it was not grief at all, but the opposite. It was, in fact, my unwillingness to grieve that had shut me down. Louise said that she did not believe her shrink's theory at first, but now she thought he might be onto something. After all, I hadn't shed a tear at Archer's funeral, and just a few mornings later I'd disappeared before dawn and come home carrying a puppy. Was Chuck some sort of substitute for Archer?

When I replied with a nasty, dismissive remark, she shook her head as though I were a lost cause and left the room. I didn't like the turn the conversation had taken. Somehow the defining moment of my adult life, my existential leap into the void, has been reduced to a discussion of my buried emotional life and psychological failings.

I wandered into the sunroom and lit another cigarette. I blew the smoke out the French doors. A muggy afternoon. I heard a noise behind me and now Louise was back, stronger and less teary, holding a glass of white wine. She said that if her therapist's theory was wrong, then what was the reason? Why had I become so cruel and closed off since Archer's death? Was it because she had been with Archer at the time he was killed? Did I blame her for it?

I looked her square in the eye. She took a frightened step

back, as though my gaze were a cocked fist. I had never said it out loud before, and I think she sensed that I was about to. I said yes. Yes, I blamed her for Archer's death. How does a mother let go of a toddler's hand in a parking lot? How could she have been so stupid?

She tried to answer, but, before she could, I was screaming at her. So much rage pent up for so long. I did not think I was capable of such ugliness. She tried to flee, but I grabbed her by her spindly wrist and threw her onto the sofa, splattering her with wine. The glass shattered against the hearth. I demanded an answer to my question. How could she have been so stupid?

She sobbed, pleading to get away. I told her that first she had to answer the question. She said that there were no cars moving anywhere. Archer wasn't a toddler. He was six. He knew about cars. She said, "Don't move," and then she grabbed the box of clothes for the charity sale. Some T-shirts spilled to the ground, and she reached for them. And that's when Susie Crater flew up on her bicycle, stoned. Who ever thinks about a bicycle hitting a child? Who's ever heard of such a thing? And Archer would never, ever have stepped into its path except that he heard the tinkle of the bike's bell and thought it was the ice cream truck.

This only made me angrier. I told her I knew it all. I had heard her pathetic story a dozen times.

"Then what do you want from me?" she cried.

"I want you to answer my question!"

"What question?"

"How you can you be so stupid? How do you live with yourself? How can you go on living being so fucking stupid?"

Her mouth fell open at my cruelty. She told me that I wasn't human. That if only I could see my face. I was a monster. She wanted me out. Out, out, out! She jumped up, her hands in my face, and pushed me toward the door. Her hatred sprayed me with spit. I did not resist or turn away. She pushed me back all the way into my study. In some strange way, her hatred excited me. She slammed the door in my face. I'm trapped here now. She has been crying on and off for the past two hours. I can hear her up there.

♦ ♦ ♦ ♦ ♦

And suddenly I am no hero, taking a bold first stride into the unknowable future. When I move out tomorrow morning, I will be just another obedient husband doing what his wife told him to do. Louise has called every shot since she ordered lunch for us that first day at the Ritz. In short, my second bachelorhood begins just at my first one ended: on my knees.

♦ ♦ ♦ ♦ ♦

As I packed my bags, Louise came into the bedroom and said that she had changed her mind, and that I could leave right on schedule, the day after we delivered Karen to college. I grabbed her by the elbow and began to apologize. She ripped her arm away and told me to save my breath. Too little, too late.

Ironically, she looks prettier and happier today than she has in at least twenty years. Is it because she is relieved to be done with me and is already planning her new life, or is it just a result of so much weeping? I guess it doesn't matter. She will do fine without me. If I am making a colossal mistake and want to return to her one day, she will certainly refuse me. I have gone and done it. No turning back. No soft landing.

◆　◆　◆　◆　◆

Just received a package from Peg. Inside were my final paycheck, a baggie of lemon candies, and an envelope— Easter egg blue without a return address. When I saw the letter inside, I instantly recognized Nora's swirly hand. Seeing the way the lines were arranged down the page, I assumed that she had finally found the courage to share one of her poems:

> I have survived so far.
> I still have night terrors.
> I can't sleep without pills.
> I am still alone.
> I still feel sad and afraid every day.
> I'm glad I'm still here.
> I have survived so far.
> I still have night terrors.

I must have read it over twenty times, trying to glean even a hint of something hopeful. It's not there. How unjust that a pure spirit like hers should be condemned to suffer like this. I pray I was not in any way the cause of it. That would be difficult to live with.

◆　◆　◆　◆　◆

I wandered into Karen's room before dinner. One look and I knew that her mom had told her everything. She pulled out her ear buds and said, "Yeah, what?" I told that I had just come to tell her how sorry I was.

She said she was not sorry at all, that it was about time I "manned up and got real."

This was not going to be the heart-to-heart I had hoped for.

"I need you to know one thing," I said. "Never in all my years of the marriage did I cheat on your mom."

"I wish you had. At least *one* of you would have been happy."

Then she jammed her ear buds back in.

When I emerged, I saw Louise through our open bedroom door, sitting at her vanity, brushing her hair, and looking particularly lithe in her silky underwear. I wandered in and asked her if she had told Sarah and Annie as well. Without so much as a glance at me in the mirror, she said that she had and that they were pretty disgusted, so I'd better wait before calling them. I asked how long I should wait. She shrugged a freckled shoulder and said, "A few months. A year. I don't know. Right now they want nothing to do with you." As I turned to leave, she added, "Oh, by the way, Annie and Joshua are engaged."

◆　◆　◆　◆　◆

I lay down on the couch and closed my eyes, thinking of Nora. After a few minutes, I heard voices, tiny, like those of a far-off radio. I couldn't identify them at first, but then I realized that they were the voices of my desperate, crazy callers. Specific lines came back to me: *I lost him to a girl with no calves. I wake up dead. He stole everything for drug money, even my diaphragm. I am a fat man. Who loves a fat man? I'm afraid to take a shower! I can't tell her that the only money we have left is in our kids' piggybanks. Why won't she love me? Why? When I was young, I was a doll. Now I'm a hag! Give me three reasons not to kill myself and I won't.*

And then with a jolt, I remembered a call that came in the morning I quit. A soft female voice. Almost a whisper. I tried to draw the woman out, but she hung up swiftly. The caller was Nora, I'm sure of it now. She recognized my voice and hung up. Perhaps she is dead already. My rational mind tells me that this is ridiculous—why on earth would she be calling a suicide hotline in a different county?—but my lizard brain can't let go of the notion. Even in hot weather Nora always buttons her sleeves to the wrist. Why? Is she concealing scars?

♦ ♦ ♦ ♦ ♦

Nora asked me the most important question of all. To whom am I confessing in these pages? The only person that comes to mind is Archer. I want him to know who his father is. This makes no sense, of course, and so the question lingers. If only I believed in God, it would be a no-brainer.

♦ ♦ ♦ ♦ ♦

The Greatest Story Never Told.

♦ ♦ ♦ ♦ ♦

I have a fantasy that on the first night I am settled in my new life, Big Peg will come over to see my place, and I will set up camp between her big, strong legs for three or four hours, devouring her. But afterward, what then? Could we have a future? She is more lesbian than straight, I fear.

♦ ♦ ♦ ♦ ♦

Without some intuitive grasp as to the value of one's own work, a writer is helpless, at the mercy of every reader's opinion, no matter how biased or stupid.

◆   ◆   ◆   ◆   ◆

A few hours ago, trying to sleep, I imagined myself on a plane bound for Oslo. When I opened my eyes, it hit me that Eva was my soul mate. Why hadn't I seen it sooner? I jumped up and turned on my computer. Without even bothering to be afraid, I went straight to the website of her charitable organization, found her name, and clicked on the tiny photo. When it blossomed to full size, I almost screamed. She had grown fat and hideous. The longer I studied the photo the more impossible it seemed that it could actually be she. I wondered if I even had her last name right. Perhaps it was actually Knudsen. Or Karlsson. This beast cannot be my Eva. Time is cruel, of course, but rarely as cruel as this.

◆   ◆   ◆   ◆   ◆

A short story where a man, using the Internet, tracks down a long-lost love, corresponds with her, and falls in love again. Only upon meeting her in Oslo does he realize that she is not the girl he knew. She is an impostor who has been afraid to tell him the truth, but he doesn't really mind, because she is even more gorgeous and delightful than the original girl. This is what's known in literary circles as a goddamn fairy tale.

◆   ◆   ◆   ◆   ◆

Who reads short stories anymore? I don't. Deep down, I hate them. It would be hypocrisy of me to write one. Unless I were certain I was reinvigorating the form.

♦ ♦ ♦ ♦ ♦

W. M. Thackeray: "There are a thousand thoughts lying within a man that he does not know till he takes up a pen."

♦ ♦ ♦ ♦ ♦

Greg Gardner is being released from the hospital today. Louise is already planning a party in his honor. I am not invited. Eavesdropping at the open bedroom door, I learned that Ellie has a guy she wants Louise to meet. I fully expected Louise to scoff at the idea and insist that it's way too soon for a fix-up. Instead, she got up and closed the door, and their conversation continued in whispers.

♦ ♦ ♦ ♦ ♦

Annie called me at three in the morning. I was wide awake and answered on the first ring. Her voice firm, she said that she was furious at me, but wanted to know what I planned to do next. I told her write a great novel. Dead silence. No encouragement at all. Not even of the insincere variety, which I would be more than happy to accept. I congratulated her on her nuptials and asked if I would be invited. She started to cry. She said no, I would not, but that I would always be her daddy and that she would always love me no matter what. I told her I felt the same way about her. Starting to wail, she hung up. I called back, but she let it ring.

◆ ◆ ◆ ◆ ◆

With the house empty this morning, I climbed up to the attic and, after an hour of hunting, found Archer's baby journals. Maybe Louise's psychiatrist was right and I had never properly grieved. What better way to begin the process, I thought, than to re-experience his short life? I intended to read all two and a half journals cover to cover, but I did not get past the second page of Book One. I have never cried so hard in all my life. I was beside myself. It took me completely by surprise. I wept and groaned. I bellowed like a wounded animal. If anyone else had been home, they would surely have called an ambulance.

Archer's baby journals are now safely stowed in my desk. I will not forget to take them with me. Once I am settled, I will read them from beginning to end, over and over again if need be, until my precious son is fully alive once more, and I lose him all over again. It will be excruciating, but I am determined to feel the loss fully this time. In doing so, I will be set free. That's the hope, anyway.

◆ ◆ ◆ ◆ ◆

This is what I was able to read of Archer's journal today before I fell apart: "Within a minute of your birth, they wrapped you up and handed you to me. You were all eyes. Huge blue eyes staring at me. I greeted you. 'Hello, Archer, I'm your daddy. Welcome to the planet earth.' Your facial expression made me think that you recognized my voice. You studied me and did not cry a peep. We stared at each other for a brief eternity. We were the only two human beings on the planet. Then I laid you in your mommy's arms, but the nurse was still tending to her, so there was no way she could give you a proper cradling or suckling. You lay there in the crook of her arm, still staring at me and every now and then trying to turn your head to look at your mom, because you recognized her voice, too, I think. You didn't look like a newborn. You looked like a wise, wrinkly, little man. Finally, I grew impatient with the delay and told the staff to hurry it up. They opened your mommy's gown, gently rolled you onto her breast, and within a few seconds you were having your first meal. I am madly in love with you. Mommy is madly in love with you. Mommy and Daddy are madly in love with each other."

♦ ♦ ♦ ♦ ♦

Why do I miss Louise so much, when she is sleeping just upstairs?

♦ ♦ ♦ ♦ ♦

This journal has at least fifty blank pages left. When I move into my new place, should I start a new one or fill this one first?

♦ ♦ ♦ ♦ ♦

A superior being from a distant galaxy lands on earth, where he is met by a spirit who offers him a guided tour of earth that he gladly accepts. Beholding humans from every walk of life, the alien is charmed by the diversity of their passions and occupations. Until at last he sees a gaunt young man, sitting alone in a barren room, staring, motionless, at a glowing screen, his brow in sweaty knots. Suddenly the young man's black-ringed eyes catch fire and, in a burst, his hands clack away at a set of tiny plastic buttons. Black squiggles squirt across the screen. Then, just as abruptly, he is motionless again. He settles back in his chair and his brow contracts.

The alien asks, "What on earth is that odd fellow doing?"

His guide replies, "He is dreaming a story. When the dream becomes real enough for him to hear, see, taste, and touch it, he records it into that machine, so that others may experience it later."

"How long until he is finished?"

"If his prayers are answered, his dreams will never cease. He will sit in that chair, week after week, month after month, year after year, until he is dead."

"Surely he is mad!" the alien exclaims.

"He would say that of us," replies his guide. "We merely endure life. He creates it."

♦ ♦ ♦ ♦ ♦

Ambrose Bierce: "From childhood to youth is eternity; from youth to manhood, a season. Age comes in a night, and is incredible."

♦ ♦ ♦ ♦ ♦

Providence tomorrow. Louise has ordered me to be on my best behavior.

♦ ♦ ♦ ♦ ♦

Louise says that when we get back she will move me into a hotel of my choosing and help me to find an apartment. She will be generous with me, she claims. I will be more than comfortable. For as long as I live, I will never have to worry about money. At long last, no obstacles. I will have nothing but time. I will be able to write to my heart's content.

THE END